Run Report 2009

ISBN 978-0-9791562-1-2

Run Report 2009:

The 2009 Collection of EMS Short Stories

THE HALIFAX EMS SHORT STORY CONTEST

Editor: Kristy Lin Billuni

Authors:

Tavi Black

Robert Evenstall

Joshua Keil

Deborah Lieberson

Ray Walker

CONTENTS

Forward
BY CHRISTINA MOORE

EMS providers see life and death differently from others. We see people at their worst and at their best. We step into people's lives at the moment when they need help. In these encounters, there are stories. We have sought out these stories and published them here for two reasons.

First, we highlight writing about EMS, a topic underrepresented in fiction. Second, we aim to raise funds for our small organization.

A few fine books have been written about EMS, and there have been some TV shows too. But in general, the EMS experience is little understood in the general population. The Halifax EMS Short Story Contest remedies this by creating a public forum for EMS literature. We received entries from across the US and entries from Canada and India. The stories represented in this inaugural edition of our collection are the best of those entered.

Halifax EMS serves the town of Halifax, Vermont. Halifax is one of the oldest towns in the state. Situated between Brattleboro and Bennington in the southern Green Mountains, we are a rural town and remote. Yes, we are within three hours of four state capitals. But we are forty-five minutes from any hospital. We have approximately eight hundred year-round residents scattered over forty square miles. Compared to Manhattan, we are nearly twice the physical size with about 0.01% of the population. We have sixty-five miles of dirt roads, no traffic lights, and one small state highway. As of the writing of this introduction, we still have a post office and a school.

To most Americans, EMS is a government service or a commercial enterprise. Here, like in other tiny communities, an EMT is a neighbor who wakes at 2:00 AM to respond to another neighbor's crisis. A call can take us four hours. We're not slow; we have to travel long distances over difficult, hilly roads.

Halifax isn't alone in these challenges. Many remote rural towns face the same issues we do. These issues are funding, access to exceptional medical care, equipment, long response times, long transport times, and a very small tax base.

Thank you for buying and reading our first edition of short stories from the contest. Your support makes a difference to the people of Halifax, Vermont. You can follow our progress, our struggles, our contest, and our future fundraising efforts through our website: www.HalifaxEMS.org.

Christina Moore is the current chief of Halifax EMS. After her return from a one-year tour in Iraq, she published her first novel entitled: *Black Swan*. During 2008-2009, Christina attended paramedic school. And now she plans on continuing her medical education – while writing and encouraging others to write.

✳

THE PRICE OF ADMISSION
BY DEBORAH LIEBERSON

With AIDS, it is often hard to know when a person needs to be hospitalized. Only in hindsight could we know when Tylenol and time would exorcise a high fever. The cough that kept Rich up half the night, was it the same cough that Ben, my two year old, had last week? Or was it the start of yet another pneumonia? Would this fever steal Rich's time, rob him of precious energy and then be gone? Or was it beginning of the infection that would take his life?

But once the decision has been made, getting a person into a hospital where diagnosis and healing can begin should be easy— or at least straight-forward. Far too often it is neither. A large teaching hospital has millions of interconnected moving parts. Some hospital gears are well oiled and move smoothly; others grind and jam. The admissions machine speeds up and slows down for reasons nobody explains to the sick or their companions. A continuous inharmonious din often makes it impossible to hear the voices of even the most committed and empathetic health care providers.

In the last year of his life, Rich was admitted to the hospital six times, spending eighty-nine days as an inpatient. There were times, when Rich was feeling better and we had had too much to drink, that we could find humor in hospital insanity. As I look back, I find it hard to remember what it was we laughed about.

For several days, Rich's fever had persisted. Despite Tylenol every four hours, it never dropped much below 101°. Sometimes, it rose to as high as 1040. After forty-eight hours of oral antibiotics, his cough wasn't worse, but it wasn't any better. For the third time in three days, Rich went to see his doctor and nurse practitioner. For reasons I cannot recall, I was not working and was with him for his appointment. Ben was in day care. Everyone agreed that it made sense for Rich to go into the hospital, where he could be given intravenous antibiotics and have diagnostic tests done more quickly.

Rich and Joan and Vicki discussed logistics. Rich could be admitted to the hospital "directly to the floor," or his admission could be done through the emergency room. After a couple of phone calls, we agreed that on this particular day, an emergency room admission would likely be the faster route.

Paperwork in hand, Rich and I left for Brigham and Women's Hospital. I pulled my car as close as I could to the door of the emergency room and looked at Rich. He opened the car door slowly. He looked pale, his skin appeared translucent.

"Let me run in and grab someone to give you a hand," I suggested. Rich wearily shook his head.

"Then at least let me get a wheelchair to bring you in."

"Deb, let me walk in myself. I'll be okay."

I had learned long ago that no amount of arguing ever changed Rich's mind once it was made up. I waited until the automatic sliding door closed behind him before pulling away.

There was a line of four or five cars in front of the entrance to the hospital's multi-tiered parking garage, which, according to a very large sign, was full. After a few minutes, one car pulled out of the garage and the car at the front of the line was allowed to pull in. I knew better than to try to find a parking space on the street. Several times in the past, I had abandoned a line assuming there had to be a space somewhere within a mile of the hospital. I was always wrong and would return to a longer line than the one I had left. After about fifteen or twenty minutes, I pulled onto the roof deck of the garage.

I walked quickly through the maze-like corridors of the hospital. I passed through the main lobby and then followed the blue lines on the wall that pointed the way to the emergency room. I had walked this same labyrinth many times before but still needed to focus on the lines or I would get lost. I saw the words, like blurry road signs along the highway, on the doors I passed: vascular surgery, infectious disease, neurology, pediatric oncology. I tried, unsuccessfully, not to look into each waiting room. Each time I did, a face would capture my attention. I could not stop myself from imagining that person's horrors, their nightmare.

I looked at my watch. I had dropped Rich off nearly a half hour earlier. I wondered if I would arrive in the ER only to find that he had already been transported up to the floor. I shouldn't have worried. When I got there, Rich was sitting with an intake clerk who was collating and stapling some of his paperwork. It didn't seem to matter that Rich had filled out the same forms less than six weeks earlier at the time of his previous admission. With the exception of the date and the reason for today's visit, nothing had changed. His address, phone numbers, employer, health insurance, next of kin, doctor, medications, and the answers to fifty or sixty other questions were exactly the same.

I sat down next to Rich. I knew by looking at him that his temperature had gone up. His skin looked pasty, his eyes glazed. He looked much older than forty-one.

"I'll take you back in just a minute, Mr. Cahalane."

"Isn't there any way they can just make a copy of the information from the previous admission and just change anything that's different?" I asked although I already knew the answer.

Rich rolled his eyes and shook his head. The clerk shrugged.

"Makes sense to me," she said. "It would make my job a whole lot easier. But nobody asks me."

She paused and looked at Rich. "I'm sorry this is taking so long."

A few minutes later, she returned with an orderly, a very tall, wide-shouldered black man who towered over us. The orderly's hospital scrubs were too short, and I could see that he was wearing white socks.

"Would you like some help getting into the wheelchair, Mr. Cahalane?"

Rich smiled weakly and thanked him. Unlike many of the doctors and nurses who told patients what to do and what they needed, this man asked and waited for a response. I knew that Rich, as I, had noticed.

I walked behind Rich and the orderly and could hear bits and pieces of their conversation. By the time he wheeled Rich into exam room eleven, Rich knew the man was from Haiti, had two young children, a boy and a girl, had worked as an orderly for over a year, and had come to the United States three years earlier. He handed Rich two johnnies. Rich extended his hand.

"Good luck, man," the orderly said as the door closed behind him.

This man had no name for us to know. The clinical staff all wore clearly visible name tags on their uniforms and lab coats. Their tags were identical: one by three inch rectangles with the hospital logo in the upper left hand corner; first name, last name, title, printed in red capital letters. The clerical staff wore smaller tags. Theirs were printed in black and had their first name, last initial and department. The transport orderly's identification consisted of a large piece of laminated plastic clipped to the waistband of his scrubs. From several feet away, when the light was not reflecting off of it, I could see a one-inch square DMV-type photo. His name probably was somewhere on the tag, but short of putting my face six inches from his crotch, there was no way I, or anyone else, could read it. Obviously, no one seemed to think that the name of the minimum wage orderly mattered to patients or staff. But it mattered to Rich, who later commented that he felt badly that he hadn't asked the man his name.

It took a long time for Rich to undress. I resisted the temptation to ask if he wanted my help. I folded his clothes and placed them in a white plastic drawstring bag that was on the gurney. We had learned from past experience that anything left behind in an emergency room was unlikely to be recovered. Rich put the first johnny on with the opening in the back and then put the second over the first, with the opening in front, tying it like a bathrobe. Veteran patients knew that this was the only way to avoid inadvertently exposing themselves while walking around. I wondered if the orderly knew this and intentionally gave Rich and others two gowns rather than one.

Rich climbed onto the exam table. After a few minutes of sitting with his legs dangling over the edge, his back unsupported, he asked me to raise the head of the table. After I did, he stretched out and closed his eyes. I realized then that I had not brought anything with me to do or to read. I closed my eyes.

About fifteen minutes passed before a medical assistant came in. She mumbled something unintelligible. The only word I recognized was vitals. The woman was massively overweight.

She moved slowly and looked down a lot. When she walked, her feet never lost contact with the floor. She looked suicidally depressed. Getting the normal, adult-sized blood pressure cuff to stay on Rich's emaciated arm was a problem. Twice it slid down to below his elbow. He grimaced but said nothing when she quickly pumped the cuff pressure up to over 200 before slowly releasing it. Her digital thermometer beeped and blinked at 103.4°. She wrote down her numbers and left without saying a word.

"Deb, can you get three Tylenol out of my bag."

I glanced at the clock on the wall but made no comment. Rich had taken three Tylenol less than three hours before. He swallowed all of the tablets at once with one gulp of water, lay back on the exam table, and closed his eyes. I stared at the ceiling and then at the floor. I looked around, desperately hoping that someone had left behind a magazine or newspaper.

The room was about nine by eleven feet and was totally devoid of color. Medical equipment adorned the institutional off-white walls. There were no photographs, paintings, or educational brochures. The floor was dark gray, speckled with flecks of black and a lighter gray. Nearly every item in the room was black, white, gray, or made of shiny stainless steel. The small, bright plastic yellow cap of some chemical solution on the counter looked garish and out of place.

There was a knock at the door, but before either of us could answer, a nurse came in. She held Rich's chart with two hands. It was at least three inches thick. The tall, thin woman moved quickly, crisply. She was either extremely efficient or cold. Or both.

"I'm Carol . . . I spoke with Dr. Goldberg earlier. She wants you admitted to infectious disease. Probably Five West. Have you been there before?"

She seemed to be asking the questions to Rich's chart. She turned the pages as she spoke, never once looking up at Rich. She didn't seem to notice or care if he answered her questions.

Yes he has, I thought to myself. Twice before. Nice of you to ask.

"There probably won't be a bed available for another few hours, so we'll keep you here. When did you last take any Tylenol?"

"About fifteen minutes ago," Rich answered.

She shook her head but made no comment. No one in the hospital had given him any, so she knew that he had taken his own. Clearly, she was not pleased.

"How long have you had the fever?" She jotted down Rich's answer. "The cough?" She wrote some more. "A medical student will be in shortly to get your history and do your admission work-up."

She knew, Rich knew, and I knew that this piece of the process could be done in less than fifteen minutes by an experienced resident. A medical student could take an hour or more.

"Would it be possible to have the resident do his admission?" I asked plaintively. "Rich has a temp of over 103°, and he feels really lousy."

"I know what his temperature is. This is an emergency room. No one here feels great. As I'm sure you know, this is a teaching hospital. Medical students are part of the territory."

Rich dozed, and I stared mindlessly at the ceiling. I looked at the clock again. One-thirty. No wonder I'm so hungry. I quietly opened the door and looked both ways, hoping to spot a vending machine in the hall. There was none. The cafeteria was in the next building, and I didn't want to leave Rich, even if there was nothing for me to do. Even with a fever of 1030, barely able to lift his head off the pillow, Rich, I knew, was a better advocate for himself than I. He had been maneuvering his way through medical mazes since childhood.

I heard Rich's chart being slid out of the box on the outside of the door. Someone turned page after page for about five minutes. Then there was a knock.

"Come on in," I said. The sound of my voice woke Rich up.

"Hi. I'm Brian . . . I'm a fourth-year Harvard med student." Brian looked at Rich. "I need to ask you some questions."

Rich suggested he pull up a chair.

"Thanks, Mr. Cahalane."

"Call me Rich."

"Okay, Rich. I'd like to start with your past medical history. I see from your chart you're a hemophiliac and have AIDS." Rich nodded.

"So, how old were you when you were diagnosed with hemophilia?"

Oh God, I thought. If he starts there we'll finish next March. I'll have died of starvation. They'll have found a cure for AIDS by then.

"I was diagnosed at eighteen months."

"Do you have any other medical problems?"

"You mean besides hemophilia, multiple orthopedic problems from the hemophilia, AIDS, and all the problems as a result of having AIDS?"

Brian's face flushed. "I guess that was a stupid question. Your medical history is just so long and complicated, I don't know the best way to start. Sorry."

"It's okay."

There was an awkward silence. Brian flipped through Rich's chart as if he were looking for something in particular, perhaps someone else's pre-admission history. He closed the volume and stared at the sheet of paper clipped to the front. It was then that he noticed Rich's vital signs.

"Did you know your temperature is over 103°?"

Rich nodded.

"You must feel awful."

"I do."

Brian looked down at his sheet of paper again. "Maybe I should start with your past hospitalizations. Can you begin with the most recent? Or maybe it would be better if I got down your medication list first."

If Brian had been one of the many arrogant, rude medical students he had had to deal with over the years, Rich would have been uncooperative and uncommunicative. But Brian's uncertainty, his honesty, and humility made Rich want to help him. Rich knew what would happen if Brian returned to the attending physician with a disjointed, incomplete medical history. Both of us had seen and heard pompous doctors criticize and humiliate medical students often in front of their patients.

"Let me see if I can give you a hand," Rich said.

Within five minutes, he provided Brian with a concise, streamlined, yet appropriately detailed past medical history and history of present illness. An experienced physician could not have done a better job. Brian scribbled frantically, trying to keep up with Rich. When he finished writing, he took a deep breath and smiled.

"Thanks. That was incredible. How'd you know how to do that so well? Do you work in health care or something?" he asked.

"Lots of practice I guess."

Brian's smile disappeared. "I guess you've been through this a lot. I really am sorry."

At that moment, Brian seemed to suddenly realize that Rich was something more than an impossibly complicated patient. For the first time, I think it occurred to him that Rich was a man not that much older than himself who was dying. He extended his hand and thanked Rich again.

"I'll try to write this up as fast as I can so they can get you up to the floor."

A few minutes after he left, Rich fell asleep. Ten minutes passed. I closed my eyes, hoping to doze off, but all I could think about was how much I wanted something to eat. And how much I wanted a cigarette.

I opened the exam room door and looked up and down the hall again. Maybe, I thought, just maybe I somehow managed to miss a vending machine the first time I looked. The hallway was eerily empty, as devoid of people as of junk food.

I looked back at Rich, who appeared to be sleeping soundly. I walked quickly to the far end of the corridor and was about to turn back when I noticed, at the far end of the next hallway, an emergency exit door that was propped open. A backpack or some sort of heavy canvas bag with a stethoscope protruding from the top was on the floor, jammed between the door and the frame.

As I got closer, I could see a pair of legs. Heavy navy blue pants looked like part of a uniform. I paused, trying to decide what to do next when, without warning, I sneezed. I was as startled as the man next to the emergency exit door. He threw down his lit cigarette, extinguishing it quickly with his shoe.

"Can I help you?" the man asked, guiltily looking around.

"Excuse me. I'm, um, sorry, I didn't mean to interrupt. I'm sure I'm not supposed to be here," I stammered.

"It's okay." He appeared quite relieved that I was not someone else.

"What are you looking for?"

"A vending machine. Something to eat. Anything."

"The closest food is the cafeteria if it's still open. Or the pizza place across the street if you have an iron stomach and love grease."

"Thanks. I should probably get back. Sorry I interrupted."

I was about to walk away but changed my mind.

"Would it be okay if I came out and had a cigarette?"

The man looked down at the pile of cigarette butts on the ground and then back at me.

"You know, this is a smoke-free facility. That means no smoking anywhere in the ER or anywhere else in or around this hospital," he said, wagging his finger close to my face.

For a moment, I was confused and a bit frightened. Fortunately, a second man, whose face I couldn't yet see, started to laugh.

"I'm guessing that the skinny-pain-in-the-ass-nurse-who-is-constantly-quoting-the-rules caught you out here again and threatened to turn you in to higher authorities, am I right?"

The first man nodded and looked back at me grinning.

"Come on out if you want."

The sudden brightness of the outdoors was disorienting and it took me several seconds to figure out that the long cement platform on which we were standing was part of the hospital's ambulance bay.

"That yours?" I asked, pointing to the nearest ambulance.

"Yep," the second man responded. He paused and took a drag on his cigarette and exhaled slowly. "I'm John, and this is Dave. "

"Debbi. I'm Debbi."

I extended my hand and looked at Dave's face for the first time. He was clean-shaven with light brown curly hair. He looked no more than twenty-three or twenty-four. I remember thinking that, despite his uniform, I could more easily imagine him as a lifeguard at the Jersey shore than as someone who dealt with car accidents and gunshot wounds.

John's cell phone rang. He smiled and walked several feet away, apparently wanting some privacy.

"So what are you doing hanging out in an emergency room on a beautiful fall day?" Dave asked.

"I'm here with a close friend who's getting admitted. The guy I live with."

"What's he in for? Hopefully, nothing too serious."

"An infection. Maybe pneumonia. He has AIDS."

"Sorry. I don't know why I asked. It's none of my business. "

"It's okay. Really."

"I can't imagine what it's like to be the person who, day after day, takes care of someone who's really sick or in pain. I don't know how people do it."

"It's hard sometimes." I paused. "The worst part is that it feels like this has been going on forever. I can't even remember when Rich wasn't sick. There are days when I feel like I just can't do this a minute longer and wish it would just be over."

I looked away, ashamed of what I had just admitted to a total stranger.

Dave lit two cigarettes and handed one to me.

"How about the person you just brought in," I asked, anxious to change the subject. "Are they going to be okay?"

"House fire. Pretty bad. Guy had second and third degree burns."

He took a long drag on his cigarette and then fixed his gaze on the wall behind me. He spoke softly, slowly. I wasn't sure if he was talking to me or to himself.

"I really hate it. The smell of burned skin, burnt hair. It's the most godawful smell in the world. And it stays with you. Even after you shower and change your clothes."

He was silent for a minute and then continued.

"Since I was a little kid, I wanted to be the guy in the ambulance—the EMT saving people. There was nothing else I've ever wanted to do. And now, I'm not sure I can do this any more. Any of it."

We looked at each other, but neither of us said a word. For a brief moment, I felt a connection to Dave, a connection that was profound and strange and intensely intimate. And then it was gone.

"Yo, Dave." John's voice startled us both. "I just got a call. We gotta go."

"Hey, you take care of yourself," Dave said without looking back at me.

"You too."

A moment later I heard doors slam and the blare of the ambulance siren. The noise and the flashing lights startled and overwhelmed me. I dropped my cigarette and squeezed back through the partially open door.

By the time I returned, Rich's chart was back in the plastic rack on the outside of the door. Brian must have finished his write-up. I sat down. A half an hour passed. Then another fifteen minutes. Afraid that we had been forgotten, I opened the door about a foot so that my chair and Rich's feet, which overhung the edge of the exam table, would be visible to anyone who walked by.

Without thinking, I pulled Rich's massive chart out of the door rack. I was curious to see how well Brian had done with his write-up. I was also so bored that I probably would have happily read the phone book if that had been the only printed material nearby. I had already counted how many holes there were in a half dozen of the acoustic ceiling tiles and calculated the average.

I read Brian's notes. Then, I read about Rich's previous hospitalizations. I read consultants' reports, nurses' notes, and discharge summaries. I was so thoroughly engrossed that I was unaware of "Nurse Ratchet's" presence until I heard her voice.

"What do you think you're doing?" she screamed as she grabbed the chart out of my hands. Rich woke up with a start.

"I was just reading—" She didn't let me finish my sentence.

"How dare you? Medical records are confidential. I don't know who you think you are, but in case you didn't know, it's against the law to—"

This time I interrupted her. "I'm sure Rich doesn't mind if—"

"I don't care if he minds or not. This is a medical record, and you have no right to touch it, read it, or be anywhere near it."

It had taken Rich a few seconds to completely awaken and move beyond his initial disorientation. His fevered lips looked painfully cracked and dry.

"It's fine with me if she wants to read my chart," he said softly.

The nurse glared angrily at him. "It's not your decision."

Rich sat up stiffly. His body posture was as close to confrontational as he could manage, and I'm sure it took tremendous effort on his part. He raised his voice only slightly and spoke slowly and deliberately, as if speaking to a child.

"Look. A patient has a legal right to have their medical records made available to anyone they want. And I'm giving consent for her to see mine in its entirety."

"If you want her to have a copy of your chart, you can go over to medical records and sign a release form."

She stormed out of the room, still clutching the chart.

"Asshole," Rich and I both said simultaneously.

We started to laugh. But within seconds, my laughter turned to tears. I was sobbing, and I didn't know why. Hot tears streamed down my face. Rich took my hand but said nothing. A short time later, a resident Rich had met before came into the room.

"Hey, I heard you two really pissed off the nurse," he said with a big grin. "Don't worry. She's an asshole. Anyway, let's get you upstairs. The folks on Five West are anxiously awaiting your arrival."

Deborah Lieberson works in education and health care. In her spare time she likes to write, grow things, take hikes, and make quilts. "The Price of Admission" was drawn from her nearly completed memoir, which explores the complex and unconventional relationship she and her young son shared with a man living with and dying from AIDS as he navigated his way through the good, the bad, and the ugly of the American health care system. Another excerpt from this memoir, "The Heart of the Matter" was published in Boston Globe Magazine. Deborah lives in Cambridge, MA.

*

SOUTH PHILLY, 1960
BY TAVI BLACK

"Ransom! Coffee!"

The forty-unit apartment building stood at the back of a parking lot, fifty yards off Washington Avenue. On the third floor, inside 33B, down the north side of the Regent Arms Apartments, Francine called out to her twenty-six year old son.

Yellow paint lines had faded on the pavement where cars parked haphazardly, leaving awkward gaps. Rusted metal railings along the shared concrete balconies gave the building the look of a rundown motel. Flights of cement stairs flanked rows of green-painted doors. Children played on the long balconies, causing women to shout at them out of kitchen windows. An empty swimming pool lay beyond the lot, fenced in and secured by a chain and padlock. Weighed down by concrete blocks, a blue tarp covered the bottom of the pool. Dead leaves and empty beer cans littered the tarpaulin.

Francine turned off the gas burner, banged the cups down on the table and called again. She wrapped her housecoat tighter and tugged on the belt. The forced-air heating escaped right out the lousy windows and under the door. Electricity prices were only going up, so she didn't bother turning the heat on until the dead of winter. Her feet were cold, and she crammed them into wooden clogs by the door. Her corns ached, and she thought about finding her slippers but turned instead to take the creamer out of the cupboard.

"Ransom! Coffee!"

She stirred the powder into her mug and then clomped down the dim hallway. On the ceiling, a round globe filled with dead flies failed to light the dirty walls, throwing only a small circle of yellow on the floor. The bathroom door was shut, and Francine smelled a sweet, medicinal scent. She heard the rhythmic whir of the bathroom fan.

"Ransom." Francine tapped lightly on the hollow pine door. "Are you sick?"

She expected a gruff answer, a curt "go away," but he didn't respond.

Francine knocked louder. Under the sound of the fan, she heard the squeal of the neighbor's plumbing, the traffic out in the street, and the shout of a man in the distance.

"Dammit. I need to use the bathroom."

Francine tried the knob. Locked. The hot sting of anger tore up from her stomach. "Open the door, Ransom. I'm serious. I swear to God if I have to come in there . . . "

She thought the door would fly open at this. He would stand eye to eye with her, his pimply face red and his harelip twitching. He would mumble something under his breath and shuffle off to his bedroom. Ransom hated when she was mad at him; even as an adult he couldn't bear to fight.

"That's it," she warned. "I'm coming in."

Francine's anger caught in her throat. The muscles constricted, and she ran to her dresser for a bobby pin. She scraped the plastic tip off with her teeth and bent the pin back. Still no sound beyond the door, Francine could hear her own breath, heavy and erratic. She poked one end of the pin in through the center of the doorknob until she felt the pop of the lock releasing. The bobby pin fell from her hand as she twisted the knob.

A wall of fumes hit her nose. Francine gagged and rose to her feet as the door swung open. "Ransom!" she shouted.

He was slumped over the bathtub, his back to the door. His bare feet stuck out from his tattered blue jeans. The skin on his soles was an unnatural color, like the purple of the dye that runs out of a new black shirt. She lunged for him. The back of his neck was covered in goose pimples. Francine screamed and slapped at his skin. His hands were stretched out in front of him like he was grabbing for the shampoo, his fingers splayed stiff except for the thumb on his right hand that clutched a rag to his palm. She tried to roll him over, but his heavy body just rocked with her tugs.

"No," she screamed. "No, Ransom, no." Francine put her hand on the back of his neck and sobbed, reaching her fingers around to the side of his neck. A faint pulse. His skin was nearly as cold as the plastic tub.

Francine heard a pounding at her front door, an insistent knock and the muffled questions of her neighbor. She knew it was Dixie. The walls were made of a thin, papery material that seemed to amplify sounds. She ran for the phone in the kitchen, her finger swirling frantically around the dial. The operator connected Francine with Pennsylvania Hospital. She gave her address. The knocking stopped though she could sense Dixie behind her, standing out on the balcony, peering in.

"Does he have a pulse, ma'am?" the calm, efficient dispatcher asked.

"Yes, I felt it."

"Is he breathing?"

"I don't know. Christ, I don't know." Francine looked down the hallway, yanking the phone cord to its limit. "Should I go check?"

"Yes, ma'am. I'll wait right here. The ambulance is on its way."

"What if he's not breathing?"

"You should resuscitate him with mouth-to mouth. Do you know how to do mouth-to-mouth, ma'am?"

Francine dropped the phone, letting the hand piece dangle from the wall.

"Franny, what's wrong?" Dixie yelled through the window.

A red gas can rested on its side on the far end of the tub. A white streak shone where the gas had trickled across the grungy floor of the tub, past the floral no-slip appliqués, cleansing a path to the drain. Francine checked under Ransom's nostrils and felt a soft trickle of air brushing against her hand.

"Thank God. Thank God," she said and tried once again to right her son. With a strength unusual for an unfit woman in her mid-forties, Francine hauled Ransom back over the tub and leaned him against the bathroom wall, his head lolling off to one side, his feet splayed out on either side of the toilet.

There was a bright rash around Ransom's mouth and rings of dirt under his nails. His fixed features expressed agony, so Francine ran her thumbs over his mouth, across his harelip, as if she might be able to mold his face into a more pleasant arrangement. She'd always felt guilty about his deformity, his cleft palate, blamed herself for drinking while she was pregnant. She yanked the rag out of his hand.

"It's for your own good," she said.

Without another thought, Francine picked up the gas can and shoved it under the bathroom sink with the rag. She grabbed a washcloth and wet it under the tap, scrubbing Ransom's face and neck, wetting his hair and lathering his hands with soap until they smelled clean. She took a towel that smelled of cigarettes and mildew off the rack and ruffled his hair, smoothing it back down after it felt dry. She kissed his hair and wiped the water from his face while tears streamed down her own.

Francine hung up the phone after the ambulance arrived. She'd stayed in the bathroom with Ransom without returning to the phone. The medical team pushed through the screen door with the gurney. Francine followed them to the bathroom and watched while they carried Ransom out and onto the gurney, fitting an oxygen mask over his nose and mouth. They asked her to step out of the hallway and give them some room.

The tallest man followed her into the kitchen. He asked her questions she didn't know how to answer. She didn't know how, what, why. She didn't know. The man's mouth twitched at the corner, and his left eyebrow slanted at an unnaturally steep angle. His brow made Francine nervous, though his manner was polite enough, and his hair was a soothing shade of gray.

"Look," he said. "I'm not going to beat around the bush. We know what your son was doing." The smell of gasoline lingered throughout the apartment. He folded his hands together in front of his crotch. "You need to tell me the truth, here. I know you've said you didn't touch anything, but I'm guessing that's not true. Did you clean up?"

"What?"

"Francine—can I call you Francine?" he asked softly.

She nodded.

"Francine. I'm not going to be delicate—there's no time for that. I know you're trying to protect your son, but the best thing you can do for him is tell the truth. Things will be much easier for all of us. I can assure you, you won't be in trouble. Do you understand?"

The red lights on the top of the ambulance circled around and around, and though the siren was off, the sound was implied in the rotating of the lights. Francine imagined the wail as she looked out over the parking lot. Neighbors stood all along the balcony and peered into her window, Dixie among them. Kids hung around the ambulance below, leaning on their bikes or circling on wooden skateboards.

"Did you clean up the bathroom?"

Francine sighed and nodded. "Under the sink." She supposed it didn't matter what happened now.

"Thank you, Francine," the man said and strode to the bathroom.

The paramedic who stood next to Ransom gave Francine a quick nod. She wondered if he'd seen many of these overdoses before; it was pretty common in this neighborhood. He looked like his job had hardened him.

Francine climbed into the back of the ambulance in her housecoat and clogs, her bushy red hair unbrushed, her face crusted with old makeup. All of the neighbors were watching. They were used to tragedy—it lived in this neighborhood, but still tragedy fascinated them, giving them something to talk about in the laundry room, on the balconies, in their dark apartments. As the ambulance turned the corner onto Washington Avenue, the driver switched on the siren. The sound matched the hammering in Francine's head, only the real siren screeched at a higher pitch than the one she imagined.

Francine called Harlee from the hospital. Her daughter was twenty-seven and lived across town, though she only came around every few months.

"Mom. I'm on my way out the door. I'll call you later."

"Your brother was taken to the emergency room."

"Ransom?" Harlee sighed into the phone. "What happened?"

"He was in the bathroom . . . I couldn't wake him up."

"Oh, Jesus. Where are you?"

"Pennsylvania Hospital. They won't let me see him."

"What did they say?"

"Nothing. There's all kinds of people. I can't get any information."

"I'll call Mickey, see if he can make it over. I'm working until four, but then I'll come straight there, I promise."

"I need some clothes."

"What?"

"Clothes. Tell your brother to bring me clothes."

No one came to sit with Francine, so she watched a TV in the corner of the waiting room. News flickered in black and white across the screen, men with crew cuts wearing dark suits interspersed with images of missiles and submarines, young black students sitting in a dime-store, refusing to move. The volume was off, so Francine stared at the images without comprehending what they meant.

She'd fallen asleep by the time a curly-haired woman shouted her name. Francine jumped and startled the child sitting next to her. She wiped drool off her cheek and shuffled forward. Where were her other children?

"You have a son here? Ransom Mahoney?"

"Yes."

"The doctor will speak with you now."

Francine followed the woman through a set of swinging doors and sat down in a small, hard chair in a tiny office. The desk and chair were made of metal and painted tan. There were no posters, no decorations in the room, just blank, colorless walls. The doctor came in shortly and gave a slight bow.

"How are you, Mrs. Mahoney? I know you've been waiting a while."

"Ms."

"Hmm?"

"Ms. Mahoney."

The doctor smiled and walked to the other side of the desk. His hands brushed back his dark hair as he spoke.

"I'm afraid the news isn't great about your son."

"What's wrong with him?"

"Ransom suffered from a severe case of hypoxia. His abuse of inhalants has caused serious damage to his central nervous system and possibly even to his heart and liver. I'm quite confident that this was not the first time. Do you know how often he used?"

"I don't," Francine mumbled.

"Ms. Mahoney, this will not be easy to hear, but your son will have permanent brain damage because of frequent inhalation of substances such as gasoline. He played a dangerous game." The doctor brushed his hair back once again. "And I'm afraid he lost."

"What do you mean?"

"Your son has lapsed into what we call a vegetative coma."

"A coma?"

"Yes, which, given time, may lead to an irreversible coma."

"Is that worse?"

"That is brain death."

Francine talked to Ransom the full twenty minutes they allowed her to sit at his bedside. His face looked calmer than it had in the apartment, with more color. She thought he looked better, his chest rising and falling with the ventilator, his eyes immobile behind dark lids. Francine took a cab home to change. The driver waited while she climbed the stairs to the apartment for the cash; she'd forgotten to bring her wallet in the ambulance. On her trip back up she saw Dixie leaning out her window. She'd be over soon.

Francine closed the apartment door. Brain dead. How could that be? Her son, her baby. She looked around; everything in her life seemed dead. A summer cactus sat on the windowsill above all of the crusty dishes and the sponge that smelled of week-old leftover Chinese. Francine couldn't remember the last time she bought a new sponge or when she'd watered the plant. She thought there must be something cursed about a woman who couldn't even keep a cactus alive.

Francine looked up at a knock on her screen door. She'd only been home three minutes, and there was her neighbor's voice, gritty with years of cigarettes and bourbon.

"Francine," her voice grated. "Honey, what happened? I saw the ambulance this morning. Is Ransom okay?"

Francine closed her eyes, hoping Dixie would disappear if she didn't answer. Dixie was always poking her nose around. When Ransom and Francine first moved into the apartment seven years ago, she thought Dixie might turn out to be a friend. They were around the same age, and she seemed like a good neighbor to have, always with news about what was happening with the other tenants, who to watch out for, who might have a little extra money and might be likely to have a neighbor over for a drink.

Two years after they moved in, she walked up on Dixie talking to Mr. Trudeau in the laundry room. Francine stopped outside the door when she heard Dixie's brackish voice say, "That Ransom of hers has got some problems."

"Oh really?" Mr. Trudeau said, but he didn't sound interested.

"Really. I think he's on some kind of drugs because I see him stumbling up the steps sometimes, always carrying bags of things in and out of the apartment."

"Maybe they're groceries," suggested Mr. Trudeau.

A dryer slammed shut, and the fluorescent light cast from inside the room flickered out across the cement walk. Francine saw their shadows stretched out long and blue in front of her from where she stood leaning against the wall, thinking that she'd been wrong: Dixie wasn't her friend after all.

"No, not groceries. I'm sure because Francine buys the groceries. I see her coming with them from Sav-Rite every third Friday when she gets her check. His bags don't have any grocery label on them, and I'll tell you what else, there's a funny smell coming from the apartment sometimes. Chemical. Like gas or something."

"A leak, maybe?" Mr. Trudeau said weakly, and there was more banging. "Well, they're all yours. Nice to see you again."

He took a left out of the laundry and almost ran straight into Francine. His eyes grew wide behind his black-rimmed glasses. He said, "Excuse me," and, "Nice evening," before he tucked his head down and shuffled past. He was embarrassed even though he hadn't said a thing wrong. Francine had never really known the quiet little man who lived on the first floor, but just then she thought she might like to. And she knew from then on she couldn't trust Dixie.

Now, standing in the kitchen, Dixie kept saying Francine's name.

"What?" she snapped.

"Francine, Lord, can I come in?" she asked though she was already sliding her slippered feet across the linoleum. "What in the world happened?"

Francine didn't answer.

"Honey, I saw them take Ransom." Dixie's lips were colored maroon, and her eyebrows were drawn in over light-beige foundation. "They had him all wired up."

"Don't you talk about him," Francine said real low.

"Now, Fran," Dixie said and put her hands on Francine's shoulders. "You sit right down here, and I'll make you some coffee. You should relax. Sit down."

Francine didn't like people touching her, especially people she wasn't fond of, but Dixie had taken her by surprise. She sat when Dixie guided her over to the chair. Something about those hands on her shoulders made Francine's eyes fill up. She couldn't remember the last time someone had touched her other than her son—the son who was in a coma. As the water started to boil in the kettle, Francine dropped her face into her hands and sobbed.

When Francine stopped crying, Dixie was sitting at the kitchen table with her. Ransom had bought the table at a garage sale down the street. "It's an early Christmas gift," he'd said as he lugged the heavy thing up the steps in September. The table with the one thick leg in the center was like an omen, Francine thought, running her hands across the nicks in the paint, because who gave a Christmas gift in September except someone who wasn't going to be around in December? Before Ransom carried the wooden table home, they had been eating off a card table that rocked if you put your elbows down on one side.

Ransom was always trying to improve their situation. He did try. Francine watched him year after year as he applied for jobs and got turned down. He was skinny as a rail with bad skin, and he mumbled if he talked at all, so much so that people always asked him to speak up or to repeat what he said. Ransom blushed but kept on mumbling. He was her youngest and the most difficult all along. It took Francine thirty-five hours to get him out of her; she was screaming bloody murder in a Pennsylvania hospital in 1934 while his military daddy headed back to base.

The doctors couldn't correct his cleft palette, so he lived the twenty-six years of his life with the top left piece of his lip smashed and dragged up towards his nostril. The kids used to tease him at school, so he just couldn't ever feel normal. He couldn't speak properly and didn't learn like the other children. There seemed to be no way for Ransom to live easily in this world. His older brother Mickey was dark and good-looking and had a cold heart from the day he was born. Mickey just couldn't be bothered with his strange younger brother, the son of a man who'd been nothing but cruel to him. Ransom's father lived with them for a few weeks here and there, when he was on leave, until he found out Francine was pregnant.

She had to help Ransom out; he didn't have the tools to take care of himself. She guessed that her other children were jealous that she let Ransom live with her, that she never kicked him out like the two of them once they got old enough to live on their own. None of their fathers were around, so she struggled to feed three other mouths all by herself. She had to let them make their own way.

His sister wasn't mean to Ransom so much as she didn't defend him. Harlee's friends would make fun of the way he talked, his fuzzy, nasally words, and Harlee giggled right along with them. Francine heard them. She heard all of them, and sometimes Ransom did too, but Francine taught him to brace himself against all that talk. She taught him how to shut out the world, all the bad shit, and look for the good.

On Sundays, Francine and Ransom would take the bus to Filter Square and go for walks down by the river, just the two of them, looking at the rowers, watching their gliding strokes in and out of the water. They stayed for hours, just watching the paddles with the water dripping off, all silent except when the blades cut back into the river. Ransom often tried to guess how many drips would come off the lead rower's handle before he put the oar back down. They almost always counted one drip, but Ransom would guess three or four every time, as if those drips held some kind of promise.

That was the good stuff. Francine knew he saw it. He'd smile when the coxswain yelled at the rowers, the little tiny person up front, facing the first in line. Ransom wondered once if Francine thought the little man ever spit in the rower's face. Francine said sure, of course, that probably happened all the time, and Ransom rolled on the grass laughing, thinking about how the rower wouldn't be able to wipe the spit off his face or he'd miss a stroke and mess up the whole boat. Ransom's face had turned red, and he had giggled and giggled.

Dixie wore floral shorts, bright blue with pink flowers that looked something like petunias, and a lighter pink top that was tight enough to show the rolls of extra skin in the folds of her armpits.

"There you are, Fran. Feeling better?" Dixie asked.

"No, not better Dixie, but I'm done crying."

"Anything else I can do for you?"

Dixie's hands were nervous, and her eyebrows kept twitching. Francine could tell that Dixie couldn't wait to ask again what happened.

"I need a highball."

"Oh," Dixie said. "Should you?"

Dixie knew Francine had quit drinking some years ago for her health—she never mentioned stopping to her, but Dixie found out, like she found out everything. Francine had contracted the gout, and the doctor had said no more alcohol. She hadn't liked quitting, but she had, for Ransom's sake more than her own.

"Yes, I should," Francine replied. "You really want to help? Run and get me a pint of whiskey."

"Well." Dixie shifted from foot to foot.

"For Christ's' sake, I need a drink before I go back to the hospital."

"Well, what—"

Francine didn't let her finish the sentence. "I'll tell you when you get back, okay? Just go."

"Um, Fran, you know I'd cover you, you know I would, today of all days, but I'm a little short," she paused. "I don't think I have enough for a pint."

"Here." Francine grabbed a twenty—part of her rent money—out of her purse. "Take it." She shut and locked the door behind Dixie.

A cockroach darted across the stove. This was what her life had come to. This was what all of her years had led up to: living in a dump all alone. This place was one of the worst she'd lived in—and she'd rented a lot of dumps—ever since she left Maine. Though Francine rarely allowed herself think back, even living in servants' quarters, being treated as inferior—often by her own family—was better than this. Here she was left with the cockroaches, the only thing that could live in such a wasteland. Once a month, they'd bomb the apartment, and the cockroaches would all run to the apartment below. Then the tenants on the first floor did the same, and the cockroaches ran back up. You can't really kill those little fuckers, Francine thought. She walked to Ransom's room and opened the closet.

She must have known what Ransom was doing all the time. She could smell it. She'd walked in on him when he thought she'd be out for the day. He hustled to hide his supplies, but she'd see his blotchy face, catch his quick, guilty motions. You couldn't hide your shame from someone who lived with you, especially from someone who birthed you. Mothers knew, even when they pretended they didn't.

"Momma," he had called from his room the week before. Ransom always called Francine Momma when he was thinking about changing his ways.

"Yeah, baby," she answered and came to lean in the doorway.

He was standing at the window, staring out at the pigeons in the old cement gulley out back, looking just like he did when he was a teenager. If she hadn't known any different she'd have thought they'd gone back in time.

"Momma," he said. "I been thinking. Maybe we should try some other town. I'm sick of this place."

"Now, just how do you think we'd manage something like that?"

"Somehow. What if we went to New Mexico? I could join the army reserves."

"What an idea. The army?"

"Wasn't my father in the military? I've been wondering if maybe that's my calling, like a family thing. It could be in the genes. Besides, they take care of you in the military."

"They send you to war."

"Not the reserves; they don't really go anywhere. You just go for a weekend here or there and then the government gives you money."

Francine walked into the room and picked up a pile of dirty clothes next to the bed. Ransom's face was red, and his forehead was coated with sweat. She carried the laundry over and used the edge of a crumpled T-shirt to wipe his brow. She couldn't tell him they wouldn't take someone like him, with a handicap. "I really doubt the military is in your genes. Besides, I take care of you just fine, don't I?"

"Yes, Momma."

"There's lots of other things we could do," Francine told him.

"Like what?" he asked.

Francine didn't give him any ideas that night. She didn't take him seriously, and now look where he was. She reached for a paper bag in the closet and knew before she opened up the folded top that it held another gas can. She sat on the floor and looked through her son's things, through all of his secrets, all of his life she felt so distant from, staying there in his room, with his things, because she couldn't imagine what else to do. Francine sat until she heard the front door rattle and remembered that Dixie was bringing her whiskey.

"Just a minute!" Francine yelled.

She quickly washed her face and threw on a knit top and jeans. She didn't want pity from her neighbor who was not her friend, so she put on the best smile possible when opening the door.

Dixie was not at the door. Francine's smile faded.

Standing in front of her were her older children, Harlee and Mickey. They were different than she remembered. It had only been four months since she'd seen her, but Harlee seemed heavier, with graying hair and lines around the edges of her mouth. Mickey suddenly looked like an adult; his chest was full, and he wore a salesman's casual clothes with a gold watch around his thick wrist. She had never known his eyes to be so honest.

"Aren't you going to let us in?" Harlee asked.

Francine unlocked the screen door and stepped aside without saying anything. She didn't know what to say. Her children filed in, and she saw that they didn't know what to say either. They stood in the kitchen with the cockroaches and looked at each other, Francine's hand on the lime green paint of Ransom's table.

"Mom," Harlee said. "We were both at the hospital looking for you."

"We saw Ransom," Mickey said. "We tried to call you."

"I didn't hear the phone," Francine said.

Two neighborhood kids walked by, looking through the blinds. They stopped and watched the strange, motionless scene in the kitchen, like Francine and her children were wax figures in a museum. It was Harlee who moved first, her makeup cracking along the edges of her eyes. She grabbed her brother by the waist and thrust him toward Francine until they were all huddled in one mass, until Francine felt the breath of her children on her neck. They were crying and murmuring, and she squeezed them tighter and tighter. The kids outside moved on, heading down to the parking lot to play Double Dutch.

"We're here, Mom," Harlee sighed. "We're here."

Francine wanted to thank them for coming. She wanted to tell her children that she needed them to be near her, but she didn't know how to say the words. Instead, she brushed her lips across the tops of their heads, standing on her toes to reach Mickey. Over his shoulder, Francine saw Dixie's bright shorts flash by the window, and in the blink of an eye she untangled herself from the cluster.

"My whiskey," she said and leapt for the door.

Dixie was there, and Francine grabbed the bottle from her, unscrewed the cap, and took a long drink before shutting the door in her face. The whiskey burned a familiar path down her throat and into her stomach, warming her skin before she turned back to her children. She glanced up at Mickey, but his face had turned back into steel, his old look she was familiar with. That was the Mickey she knew. But his sister too had stopped crying. Harlee wore a self-righteous scowl.

"What?" Francine said, but she knew.

She knew that it was grief or grace or even God that tore down the walls between them for just a minute or two, a moment that would probably never be regained. Her children did not like her. That was okay. That was okay, she told herself and took another drink of whiskey.

Tavi Black is a writer and a painter living with her husband on Vashon Island outside of Seattle. She recently graduated from Lesley University's Low Residency MFA program in Cambridge, MA. She has worked as a ballroom dance instructor, a producer, a stage manager, and a lighting technician. She toured the world with groups such as Phish and Norah Jones before working up the nerve to go back to school and pursue writing. She is currently working on both a novel and a memoir of her years on the road. Her story "Notes from a Female Roadie" was a finalist for the 2008 Glass Woman Prize. Look for her short story "The Flame" in the summer 2009 issue of *Alligator Juniper*.

Man Down
by Joshua Keil

They arrived at the designated apartment with Engine Two right behind them. A policeman told them to wait outside. The police broke the lock on the front door and entered the apartment, pistols drawn.

While the other medics and firefighters waited, Eric grabbed the airway bag and the heart monitor from the back of the ambulance, clenching them both until his knuckles whitened. He had just earned his EMT certification from a college class, and this was his first 911 trauma—a "man down"—the most ambiguous kind of call there was. Neighbors reported screams from inside the apartment and visible blood on the floor through the window. No one knew what had happened. The rescue workers, equipment in hands, eyes fixed on the apartment building, knew nothing about what the next few minutes might bring.

A female police officer appeared at the front door and yelled, "All right, guys, get in here!"

The group moved rapidly with their equipment into the apartment. A feeble light squeezed into the dark early autumn morning. Eric noticed the recently well-decorated and clean interior, and a smashed lamp on the floor, an overturned shelf, and knickknacks strewn around the living room. Dried blood streaks stained the carpet, the kitchen counters, and the walls. Down the narrow hallway, there were more streaks, as if someone had taken a paintbrush back and forth, back and forth. In a back room, Eric heard a struggle, and a man screamed. "Help me! Heeelp!" a guttural, wet voice yelled. Was it too late to turn back? Maybe this EMS gig wasn't for him.

In the bedroom, Eric, his partner, Tim Adler, and several firefighters found a tall middle-aged man in nothing but his underwear, wrestling on a large bed with the policeman. Dried, cracked blood plastered his face, chest, and hands. The policeman was on top of him, pinning his arms down, trying to calm him.

Tim took charge while the entire group rushed to hold the man down. "Sir, we're trying to help you! Calm down! Calm down! Stop moving! Sir, what's your name? Sir, can you hear me? What's your name?"

The man never answered. Completely detached from his surroundings and possibly even from himself, he kicked and pushed and would not respond with anything but cries for help. On closer look, fresh, barely coagulated blood ran down his chin and neck. Gurgling noises came from his throat. His bruised left eye bulged from its socket, but it was difficult to assess the cause or extent of his injuries. Panic-stricken, he continued to resist help, even though he pleaded for it.

Tim gave orders, "Okay, let's get this guy on the backboard and strapped in, even if it's just to restrain him."

One of the firemen who had carried in the long, yellow spine board laid it next to the patient while the others held onto the patient's body.

"On the count of three, let's roll him and do a back check. One . . . two . . . three."

While trying to keep the patient's spine straight, Eric and the three firemen, including the fire-medic, Sheila Olson, rolled the patient onto his side while Tim quickly examined his back for injuries. "Okay, clear," he reported.

The man still resisted but with less force now. He still screamed for help. The group rolled him back onto the long board, and Eric grabbed the Velcro spider-straps to immobilize the patient against the board. He did it in mere seconds.

Tim continued the assessment. "Okay guys, let's find out what's going on here!" His voice was not calm. Eric understood; no one was calm. No one knew what was wrong, and the patient was not able to explain a thing. "Let's get a blood pressure. And check for other injuries!"

Tim shined his penlight into the patient's eyes. The right was barely responsive, and the left one protruded almost completely out of its socket, staring dead off into space. One of the firefighters loosened the straps around the left arm to get a blood pressure. Eric and the others checked the rest of the body for injuries and prepared the oxygen.

"He's got a lot of blood in his throat," Sheila, who was also at the head, said after looking in the mouth. "Some of this blood is real old, but there's fresh stuff too!"

"He's bleeding a little from his eye. Where's the rest coming from, guys?" Tim asked. He and Sheila were having a hard time holding the patient's head still. He coughed and sprayed blood, some of it on their shirts and faces. Eric didn't like the feel of this at all. It was messy and confusing.

"There's nothing down here!" Eric reported. "I'll go get the cot ready."

"Okay. Where's the oxygen?"

"Here!" Sheila handed Tim the mask while another fireman connected the tubing.

"Fifteen liters?"

"Yeah. Looks like there's a wound under his chin. What's his pressure?"

Two firemen had been working unsuccessfully at the blood pressure on his free arm, but that arm, now free of its straps, was not cooperating. "Just a second!" one of them said.

"I need it now!"

One firefighter tried to pin the arm still. The other listened with the stethoscope while letting the pressure hiss out of the cuff. The fire captain, meanwhile, had just finished applying heart monitor electrodes to the patient's bare chest.

"Just palpate the pressure if you need to!" Tim used an alcohol wipe to clear the dried blood from under the patient's chin.

"Pulse of seventy. Respirations twelve," Sheila told the fire captain, who wrote the information on a pad. "Still waiting on the pressure."

Eric came back through the door. "The cot's right outside the front door. It'll be easier just to carry him out on the board!"

The fireman took the stethoscope out of his ears. "Pressure's eighty over forty!"

"Do you want me to intubate this guy?" Sheila asked. She was trying hard to keep the oxygen mask over the patient's nose and mouth, both of which both moved despite the straps.

Eric noticed the patient moving less since he'd left for the cot. He now only groaned. The struggling must have taken a lot of energy out of him, or the straps calmed him, or both.

Tim didn't hear Sheila's question about intubation. "What's this, Sheila?" Tim had cleared the blood from under the chin and exposed a small, bleeding hole. "Is this what I think it is?"

Sheila palpated the wound with the tip of her gloved finger. The others stopped to look. She turned to the policeman standing behind the others with his flashlight and said, "Look for a gun!"

The police and some of the others began looking around. Sheila suctioned blood from the patient's mouth every time he began to gurgle again. Already, the suction container had an inch of blood in it.

"Here's a spent case!" The policewoman had found something on the floor. "It looks like a twenty-five caliber." She held the tiny brass cartridge up to the light.

Tim finished applying a C-collar around the patient's neck, and Sheila held the head with her free hand. "Careful guys," Tim said. "We don't know where that bullet ended up, and I don't see an exit wound anywhere." Eric heard the slightest shake in Tim's voice.

Sheila again went back to the airway issue. "We're gonna have to do something about his airway, it's getting worse!"

"I know. Let's get this guy movin' first! What was the second pressure?"

"Still eighty!" The fireman reapplied the spider-straps on that arm.

"Let's go, guys! Are we ready?" Everyone positioned themselves around the backboard and slung equipment, oxygen tanks, and the heart monitor over their shoulders.

"Is the cot ready, Eric?" Tim obviously hadn't heard the first time.

"Yeah, it's outside; the hallway's too narrow!"

"Okay, on the count of three. One . . . two . . . three!"

The group of five lifted the patient from the bed. On one side, those lifting crouched on their knees, duck-walking across the mattress. The patient coughed again, blood spluttering out from the hole in the flesh under his chin. They started walking, and Tim cleared dried blood from the patient's injured left eye.

"Do you think the bullet exited there?" Sheila asked, gripping the board with one hand and suctioning the patient's mouth with the other.

Tim replied, "No, I don't see where it came out. I think it could be in his eye though, or at least hit the back of it. It's probably sitting right behind his eye."

"Or further back," Sheila said. "It's a small bullet; it wouldn't necessarily kill him."

Eric's mind wandered when he again saw the blood streaks in the hallway and the broken lamp in the living room. He noticed blood in the bathroom, and as they passed the kitchen counter, he saw a broken picture frame and a picture of the patient. In it, the barely recognizable man smiled and held a woman's hands. They looked happy.

"His name is Russell!" the policeman looking through the patient's wallet said.

"Russell, can you hear me!?" Tim yelled in the patient's face. No response. Though no one had said it yet, everyone knew this was a suicide.

"When do you think this happened?" Eric asked.

"Probably some time last night," Tim replied, distracted and jittery.

The group was outside now. They loaded the patient onto the cot that Eric had already lowered to the appropriate level. The policewoman made the crowd of bystanders back up.

"Okay, Sheila, how's his breathing?" Tim asked.

"Not good; there's a lot of blood in his throat. I need to start bagging him to get some air into his lungs."

"Okay, wait'll we get inside the truck!"

One of the firemen opened the ambulance doors, and the others slid the cot inside. Sheila took her place in the jump seat at the patient's head, and Tim sat on the long bench beside the patient.

"Okay, Eric!" Tim yelled out orders while Eric loaded bags at the side door. "Get another fireman in here for the trip. And tell the captain that Sheila's comin' with us!"

"Roger!"

One of the firemen, Tyrell, overheard and jumped in beside Tim. Tim instructed him to hold the patient's legs since he was growing more resistant again. As soon as all the equipment was inside, Eric asked, "Tim, you guys need some help now, or are we goin'?"

"No, get in here first and get Sheila a BVM!" Eric climbed in even though he had to stand halfway into the small passage that led to the front cab. The back of the van-type ambulance was getting crowded. He reached for the bag-valve-mask under her seat.

"Let's start an IV!" Tim yelled. Eric turned to prepare the IV fluid. Tim's voice was still shaky.

Sheila said, "Tim, you know what we're gonna have to do here. He has a hole in his chin and tongue, and another in the roof of his mouth, and it's all full of blood." Sheila's voice trembled a little too. Eric hoped the tremor in their voices was from adrenaline and not uncertainty.

"I know," Tim said. "We're gonna have to tube him. I was hoping we wouldn't have to paralyze him though. What do you think? He's still really active and still gagging!"

"I think we're gonna have to! It's not gonna be an easy tube. I don't think he'll take the tube down if we don't R.S.I. him."

"Okay, you're probably right. I hope you're up on it, Sheila! I've looked at it, but this will be my first time for Rapid Sequence Intubation! Eric, you got my tape ready?" Tim wiped a vein on the patient's arm with an alcohol pad.

"No!" Eric was still bleeding the air out of the IV tubing, laying it close to Tim. "I'll have it in a second!"

Sheila dug her intubation kit out of her own bag with one hand while still pumping breaths into the patient every three seconds with the other. "Eric, can you crack open the R.S.I drugs?"

"Just a second!" Eric finished the tubing and handed a roll of tape to the fireman holding the legs to save time. "Can you rip four pieces and hang them up there?" Tyrell was eager to have another job, and it freed Eric to get the drugs.

Tim had the needle and catheter and was ready to puncture the man's vein. "Man, guys, I don't know about this." His voice was shaking with more trepidation. "This guy has nothing for veins."

Eric and Sheila both looked at the arm, but they didn't have to. They knew, with a pressure of eighty, it would be difficult.

"Yeah." Sheila tried encouraging him. "But you've got it, Tim."

While Eric prepared the drugs, following Sheila's instructions, he pondered how strange it was they were making so much effort to save a man who obviously didn't want to live. It was a strange feeling. He hadn't pictured emergency medicine to be like this.

Despite all signs to the contrary, Tim hit the vein. "Okay, I've got a flash. Where's the tubing?!" Tyrell handed it to Tim. Tim hooked up the tubing and instructed the fireman to open up the line.

"Okay, we're good!"

"Good job, Tim!" Sheila said. She assembled the laryngoscope and checked its tiny lightbulb.

Eric watched the patient's body grow more pale and the gurgling noises more muffled each time Sheila squeezed the bag.

Handing the first syringe to Tim, Sheila said, "I figure he's a hundred kilos, so here's twenty milligrams."

Tim paused, holding the syringe needle next to the IV port. "Are you sure we need to do this? It might be best to wait to do anything dramatic. Because once we do this, you've got to be able to get that tube in or we're screwed!"

"I will." Sheila looked down at the oxygen saturation level on the pulse-ox. "His O2 saturation is down to eighty-eight percent."

Eric knew the difficulties they faced. The patient grew less and less able to breathe on his own. On top of that, the breaths he could take were merely sucking blood into his throat. That's why he needed to be intubated: to have a long plastic tube inserted directly into his windpipe where an air-filled cuff would prevent blood from passing. However, the patient was still conscious enough to have a gag reflex and resist the tube, so he needed to be paralyzed first. That's what the R.S.I. protocol was for. The drugs would relax his gag reflex, completely paralyze him, and stop his breathing, making it easier for Sheila to use the bag to give full, deep breaths and possibly save the man's life.

"Okay, here goes." Tim applied the syringe to the port, the end of the needle quivering slightly. As he slowly pushed the syringe, the others watched the drug take effect. Sheila held the laryngoscope, ready to insert it into the patient's mouth to lift his tongue. In her other hand, she held the tube she would insert into the windpipe, but she had to wait.

Over the course of several seconds, the drug worked down the patient's body. First, his face relaxed, followed by his neck and upper torso. At this point, the patient would be able to remember the events, that is, if he didn't suffer permanent brain damage. But Eric knew that the next drug, Versed, would erase his memory. Arms nearly flaccid, his breathing slowed, and the gurgling noises grew more muffled and less frequent.

"Oh, shit!" Tim began to tape the catheter to the patient's arm when the arm suddenly jerked, pulling the catheter from the vein with some of the drug still in the tubing. "Shit, shit, shit!"

Now Tim and Sheila both were markedly nervous. The patient had been given only a half-dose of the first drug in the series. He was just half-paralyzed, and neither medic was sure they would be able to establish another IV. Tim had been lucky the first time.

"Okay, Sheila, tube him!" Tim yelled. "Eric, let's go! Lincoln General!"

"Right!" Eric jumped out the side door over four large equipment bags. He was glad to leave the situation inside. He knew, though, that he would have to get them to the hospital fast. Tim's voice sounded defeated already, and Sheila was becoming a nervous wreck.

Eric asked the female police officer to guide him while he backed up the ambulance, then went quickly around to the driver's door. One of the still-present firemen asked Eric, "Why haven't you guys left yet?"

"I don't know," Eric replied as he climbed inside. "Ready?" he yelled back.

"Yeah! Go, go!"

Eric flipped the switch that returned the engine to a normal, slow idle, and radioed dispatch. "Dispatch, Medic Three."

"Go ahead, Medic Three."

"Medic Three en route Lincoln General, code three, advanced life support."

Eric put the ambulance in gear, flipped on the siren, and drove toward the hospital. He listened to the conversation in the back.

"Tim," Sheila said. "Can I get some suction?" Eric heard the purr of the vacuum unit sucking blood out of the patient's mouth.

In his mind, Eric wondered why Tim still called him "the patient." His name was Russell; that's what the police officer said. Russell. Russell what? he wondered.

"Man, I can't see anything!" Sheila sounded like a woman who could feel a serious situation slipping away. She pushed the tube blindly.

Russell was not doing well.

"I think you're in the esophagus," Tim said.

"Shit! Are you sure?"

A few seconds passed. "Yeah, I'm sure."

Even with his lack of experience, Eric knew that everything was going wrong with the call. They had paralyzed the patient who, consequently, hadn't had a breath for nearly a minute. His brain was probably starving for oxygen. Maybe they should never have paralyzed him, Eric thought. Maybe they should have done nothing at all. When they'd arrived at the apartment, the man was walking. Talking, even! "Help me," he'd yelled and moaned. He had obviously been like that all night, and now he was close to death.

All night! Eric thought about that again. What a nightmare! At some point in the middle of the night, this man, Russell, put a small-caliber pistol under his chin and pulled the trigger. The bullet easily passed through the flesh under his chin, through his tongue and the palate above, until it rested somewhere behind his eyeball. What happened next was not what Russell had planned—he didn't die. Not even close, really. He'd become disoriented. He apparently didn't know who he was or what had happened. He was semi-conscious, scared, walking around the house, bleeding from somewhere, perhaps acting out of instinct, and not knowing what to do. Something deep within him knew only to call out for help.

Though the trip took no longer than five minutes, it seemed to last forever. Eric could hear the situation unfolding in the back. Sheila attempted a crichothyrotomy. She cut a hole in his neck because they'd obviously never gotten the airway tube in.

Tim then used his portable radio to contact the emergency room doctor. As he gave his dismal report, Eric zoned him out. For just a minute, he forgot about the drugs and the crichothyrotomy. Tim's agitated voice and the wail of the siren faded. Instead, his mind gave full attention to what had happened to the patient.

What was his name again? Russell? Why did he shoot himself? Eric could not imagine such sadness. What's more, there was probably a bullet in his brain ruining his thought processes and shattering any sanity he had. Eric wondered what it was like when Russell found himself in a half-conscious world. He might have even thought that he actually had died. He only knew the blood, the walls he kept running into, the blindness, the confusion, and the pain. Perhaps he thought he was asleep, having a nightmare. Or, God forbid, he thought he was dead and in some kind of hell.

Perhaps he thought he had become a spirit wandering his apartment. Some deep animal instinct told him that he needed help, so he cried for it. Then, strange hands wrestled with him. He did not know the hands all over his body were good hands, were friendly hands. They were not the hands of demons dragging him down. They were the hands of policemen, medics, and firemen.

Only a few minutes later, Eric cut the siren and pulled into an inviting place—the Lincoln General Emergency Room. Under the awning of the emergency room garage, Eric killed the engine, flipped the main battery switch, and jumped out. When he opened the back doors, the fatigue hit him. It seemed like he had been on this call for days. Sheila and Tim were having some sort of argument about a tracheotomy or something.

"That's too low!" Tim was saying. "That's not a crich, that's a trach. We can't do that!"

"Look, Tim, you're the lead medic here. I just want to say for the record that I have no responsibility in this matter. I just followed your lead."

"What the hell are you talking about, Sheila?!" Tim exclaimed. "I wasn't the one chomping at the bit to R.S.I. this guy."

The argument might have worsened, but the doctor ran up beside the cot. Eric walked away. Twenty-five minutes ago, they'd found a man walking around his apartment. Now they had some sort of half-dead vegetable on their hands. This was not at all what he thought emergency medical calls would be— not at all! Had they really helped the man? Did he want to be helped? Did they save his life? Did they make him worse? Is this the way it always was? The only solace Eric found was just an hour remained of his shift. He could go home and sleep and hopefully forget about this, but he was skeptical about that.

At home, he tossed and turned, trying to think of peaceful things and happier places. Oddly enough, he even tried to think of his classes and the exams coming in a few weeks. Nothing worked. Was Russell dead? Dear God, was Russell in a coma? Was he, Eric, partly to blame for this?

It was strange walking into the ICU in plain clothes, coming to visit a man he didn't know. "Russell Baxter?" he said to the receptionist at the central desk. She frowned and pointed to a corner room. "How's he doin'?" Eric asked her.

"You'll have to ask the nurse. She's in there."

Eric almost turned around, but something pushed him on. He had to find out what happened. He had to make sense of this. He thought medicine was going to be his career. This was about his life too.

The room was nearly dark inside. Russell lay sleeping or comatose on the bed. He had a bandage over most of his head, including his left eye. He was cleaned and shaven and hooked to a respirator beside the bed. A nurse pushed buttons on an infusion pump, and one of the police officers from earlier in the day sat nearby, writing notes.

The nurse turned toward Eric when he stepped inside. "Can I help you?" she asked.

"I . . . I just came to see how he's doing," Eric said, pointing toward the bed. "I'm one of the medics who picked him up."

The nurse's face softened once she heard he was a medic. "Oh, hi, I'm Janice," she said, extending her hand to him. She was perhaps in her early forties, plain-looking, but nice. The policeman merely nodded at him with something similar to a friendly smile.

"I'm Eric," he said.

"Pleased to meet you," Janice said. "You're pretty young, Eric. You been working at Eastern Ambulance for very long?"

"No, just started actually. Just a few weeks. I'm a university student; I do this part-time."

"Oh, I see." She fumbled with something in her pocket. "So, you've come to see Russell?

"Yeah. Just wondering how he's doing?"

"He's doing good," she said, placing qualified emphasis on the word, good. "It looks like he's made it past the worst part."

"Did he have surgery?"

"Yeah, they ended up removing his eye. It was destroyed."

"Wow. That's too bad," he said. "I was worried that would happen. Is that where they found the bullet?"

"No, actually, the bullet was in the back of his brain."

"What?" he said.

"Yeah, sounds kinda crazy, huh? It went up behind his eye, then bounced off the back of his forehead, and went almost clear through his brain."

"Oh my God!" Eric said. "Are you serious? I didn't even know someone could live like that!"

She looked at Russell in the bed. "Apparently, they can. They said it was a small bullet. I guess it's not like the movies, huh, where all the bad guys die with one shot?"

"Sometimes they do," the policeman said. "But sometimes they don't." He stood up and offered his hand to Eric. "Jeff Thornton," he said.

Eric shook his hand. "Eric Wright." Eric shoved his hands back into his pockets and looked around like he didn't know what to do next.

"Do you wanna sit down?" Janice asked.

"Sure," Eric said reluctantly. He looked again at Russell. "So, is he in some sort of coma?"

She grimaced. "Yeah, it seems like he probably is. He's still recovering from surgery, though."

"So you think he might wake up?"

"Dr. Green says probably not. Too much brain damage, you know."

Eric nodded and said to Jeff, "Suicide?"

"Yeah. Pretty straightforward. Left a note."

"A note?"

"Yeah, found it on the kitchen floor."

"What did it say? Or can I even ask that?"

"I don't see why not. Just the usual stuff, that he still loved his wife who was cheating on him and just asked him for a divorce. Said he was willing to forgive her but realized she was never coming back. Couldn't stand living without her." The policeman finished his account as quickly as it began. That must have been all there was to the note.

Eric was depressed. He was too sensitive, he told himself. "He was married?" he said, not really as a question.

"Yep, still is. Wife came in this morning."

"What did she say?"

Jeff pursed his lips. "Didn't say too much, really. She was here with her boyfriend, I guess. He waited outside. She asked about his prognosis, asked a lot of questions, and said she'd be back later."

"What is his prognosis?" Eric asked.

Janice answered that one. "Machines. He'll be on the vent for the rest of his life and will need full-time care. He can't live without a respirator. He was on one before he even went into surgery."

Eric sank back into his chair. He stared at Russell with the strange feeling that he was Dr. Frankenstein staring at a monster he had just created. Machines? Machines? Is that what they'd worked so hard for? So, that was it?

Officer Thornton spoke again. "The wife wants to turn off the machines."

Eric was dumbfounded. "What? So soon? She just found out about him this morning. Does she really have a say in that?"

"She might," was all Jeff had to say. "She's still his wife."

Eric hadn't known what he would find when he got to the hospital. He asked himself what it was he wanted to find, but the answer was absurd. Of course he wouldn't find this man awake and whole. Of course there would be no man named Russell here to say thank you. That was what Eric wanted, though, wasn't it? That's the way things were supposed to work. When you provided medical care to someone, especially advanced life support, it was something they really needed—something that could really help. There was none of that here. Russell didn't want help. Russell was trying to die. Eric, Tim, and Sheila had made gargantuan efforts that merely starved his brain of oxygen and ensured that Russell would live on machines.

Jeff Thornton got up to leave. Janice walked by Eric's chair and asked if he was going to stick around.

"I . . . I don't know," he said.

Janice looked at Eric sympathetically and said, "Dr. Green will be in later, and she can answer your questions much better than I can."

"She will? Well, I don't know if I have any more questions. I'll just hang out here a bit and take off in a minute."

"Suit yourself," she said. "Let me know if you need anything. I'll be right outside."

"Sure," Eric said. "Thanks." It was a strange feeling. Suddenly, he was being treated like a family member, like someone who was going to stay and wait it out with Russell. The strangest thing about it was that it somehow felt right.

Janice dimmed the lights as she went out. Eric rested his head on the back of the patient recliner and stared at the ceiling.

"Where is your family, Russell?" he asked. "Don't you have anyone? I mean, I know about your wife, or ex-wife, or whatever she is. I thought there might be others, though." Eric looked out the open door like he half-expected more people to come in. "I didn't mean for you to turn out like this, ya know. I know this isn't what you wanted, but it's not my fault. You need a bigger gun."

Eric felt ashamed for saying that. He felt his eyes grow tired. He closed them and rested his head all the way back. "I'm sorry. I didn't mean that. Maybe you did that on purpose. Maybe you weren't really sure you wanted to die, so you kind of did it halfway. Maybe you want to live, still? Is that true?" He leaned his head forward and looked at him again. Only the repetitive hiss-and-thud sound from the ventilator filled the silence. After a few seconds, he closed his tired eyes. "Look at you, Eric. You're totally crazy! What are you doing here, anyway? That nurse probably thinks you're a psych case, too. Russell's not going to talk to you."

There was a blanket folded on the arm of the chair. Eric was cold. He unfolded it and covered up. The chair wasn't too uncomfortable, and the room was nice and dark. "Eric, calm down," he said. "You're not crazy. You're just tired. You're just checking on a patient." Within minutes, he was asleep.

He awoke from a deep sleep to voices, two women. His eyes opened to the sight of the beige-colored wall, and his head had fallen over to nearly rest in his shoulder. He had a terrible kink in his neck. He raised his head painfully and slowly and saw Janice talking to an older woman with long hair and intense concentration in her eyes. The new woman asked about the PEEP settings on the vent.

"He seems to be doing well on this," Janice said.

Beyond them, the view from the seventh-story window showed Eric that the day had faded to evening. He had been asleep for hours. Great! These people are really going to wonder about me. They're going to think I've been overly traumatized by this call. Then the disturbing thought hit him that he was overly traumatized by the call. If not, he wouldn't be in here. It was rather embarrassing, he thought. It definitely showed him to be an overly sensitive novice.

"There's a tray there for you," Janice said. Eric looked up at her and realized the two were now looking at him. She indicated a tray of hospital food on the stand next to him.

"Oh . . . wow. Geez, I must have been asleep for quite a while. Working long hours, I guess. I totally didn't mean to stay here. I was just going to—"

"Well, aren't you hungry?" the other woman said.

"Yeah, I'm starved."

"Then help yourself. You need to eat. I'm Dr. Green."

"Hi, I'm—"

"Eric," she answered for him. "I know. You're one of the medics that brought Mr. Baxter in. Janice told me."

"Yeah, that's right. Are you his doctor?"

"I'm one of them. He's had plenty of doctors since he arrived this morning."

"Yeah, I bet."

"Poor guy," she said, looking at his face. "Tough, tough case, this is."

"Yeah, it's sad all around," Eric said, sitting up from his reclined position. "What's gonna happen to him?"

"That's a very good question, Eric, one that I'll be thinking about quite a bit."

"I heard his wife said we should turn off the machines?"

Dr. Green bit her lower lip while thinking. "Yeah, that's what she said."

"Is she the one who decides?"

"No, not really. But she is his wife, albeit estranged, and her opinion carries a lot of weight in this case. Plus, she said that

Russell had expressly told her several times that he never wanted to be kept alive by tubes and machines. That is a form of an advanced directive, albeit a verbal one."

"But other people decide too?"

"Yes, you could say that."

"Who?"

"Me, the ethics committee, and his other doctors." Dr. Green walked over to the window, leaned against the wall, and fumbled with her necklace as she looked out.

Eric got up, joined her by the window, and looked out over the city. From that vantage point, he could see all the way to the state capital building in the early evening light. The autumn trees had lost their leaves, and the city looked gray and lifeless. That's how Eric felt inside. It was then he realized this story would not have a happy ending. He remembered a dream he had in the reclining chair. Russell's wife and family came to the bed. Some woman—his mom, perhaps—leaned over him to stroke his forehead and say her goodbyes. But that was just a dream.

Why was he hanging around? He wanted closure, he realized, and it wasn't coming. He waited to see if their life-saving efforts gave Russell a second shot at life, a chance to make peace with God, or at least an opportunity for his family to see him and say goodbye. Do medics fight just to give someone the opportunity to live in a coma, especially when no one, not even the patient, wanted him to live?

"Don't you just keep him alive whenever you can?" Eric asked, turning to the doctor.

Dr. Green was a caring, intuitive person, and very intelligent. Eric could see that in a minute, and he gravitated toward that wisdom. "Eric," she said, turning her gaze toward him. "There's something you need to understand."

"What's that?"

"Something happened thirty or forty years ago. Something very big. It was a huge change for humans and especially for medicine."

"Technology?" he guessed correctly.

"Yeah," she said. "That's the easy part, but the difficult thing to see is the change that technology has brought about. I'm talking about what it did to medicine and our decisions about life. Throughout all of human history, medicine was simple—do everything you can to keep the patient alive, even when there wasn't much to do. There weren't many tough questions. We studied and studied and did everything we could to sustain life. Country doctors out on the prairies did this. Surgeons in city hospitals did this. It's just that no matter how hard we tried back then, some people lived and some people didn't. We did our best, and we couldn't control the outcome.

"But now—" she took a deep breath and rolled her eyes. "Now, we've got a big problem. We've created machines that . . . what do they do? Do they keep people alive? They keep oxygen flowing to all their tissues; I can say that for sure. Are they alive? Is Russell alive? Well, technically, I think the answer is yes. But is he really alive? We've done everything we can for him, I think, but he's not going to get any better. In fact, if anything, he's getting worse. The most recent CAT scan shows two expanding hemorrhages, but they might stop. They might become controlled on their own after causing perhaps more brain damage. But the injuries that normally tell a body to shut down can't do that unless we let them."

Eric thought about this for a moment. "You're basically saying we've gotten so good at keeping people alive, we don't know if we've gone too far?"

She looked out the window and furrowed her eyebrows. "Maybe, but perhaps you're still not getting the central point, Eric. Think of it this way. We can basically take a corpse, someone who has actually died just recently, hook them up to a heart and lung machine, a dialysis machine, and whatever else they need to keep their tissues alive. Do you see what I'm saying? We've completely destroyed the old paradigm. In the past, all our efforts were to preserve life. Now, we have to decide what life is, and we don't know! It's muddy, muddy, muddy, and nobody likes it."

This was strange, Eric thought. He understood we now had amazing technology, but he had never understood what that actually meant. The question had changed somewhere along the line from how to keep someone alive to how long. Along with that question came the related questions of by what means, to what extent, and perhaps the worst, whether we cause suffering rather than alleviate it.

Eric pinched the bridge of his nose and stretched the skin on his cheeks. He was trying to wake up. He was trying to avoid thinking.

"So, what do you think's really gonna happen with Mr. Baxter?" he asked.

She took a deep breath. "Mr. Baxter will continue like this for a few weeks. His wife will be asked about her thoughts and what, specifically, her husband said about not wanting to live on machines. She might talk to one of our chaplains or a psychologist. We'll look at his CAT scans and brain scans and try to determine if he's improving or not and whether he's in a persistent vegetative state. The ethics committee will discuss the legal implications and document Mrs. Baxter's statements. Eventually, we'll turn off the ventilator, and if that doesn't end it, which it will, we'll start to turn off nutrition and hydration too." She stopped and thought for a moment. "I hope it goes that smoothly," she said. "I hope it doesn't go to court. When the lawyers get involved, it cheapens things so much."

Eric had no response. He'd had no idea that their actions this morning would lead to such a heart-wrenching, drawn-out process.

There was a knock on the metal doorjamb of the ICU room. "Visitors," Janice called in.

Dr. Green and Eric turned. A long-faced woman with a protruding nose entered the room cautiously. Eric noticed she avoided looking directly at Russell. An older woman, who looked much like her, but overweight, followed close behind.

The older woman, however, certainly looked at Russell, and when she did, it was in stone-faced shock mixed with some revulsion.

"Hello, Charlene," Dr. Green said.

"Dr. Green, it's good to see you again. You've already done so much to help us through this difficult time. I want you to meet my mom, Beverly." They shook hands. "How's he doin'?" this woman, presumably Russell's wife, said without looking at him.

"He's about the same as he was this morning," Dr. Green said. "There's been one change. It appears two of the many hemorrhages in his brain may have grown larger."

"Oh, that's bad, isn't it?" Charlene asked.

"Yes, it will be if they don't stop. They could cause further brain damage."

"Well, from what I understand, there's not much brain left to be damaged. Isn't that so?"

Dr. Green played with her necklace again and spoke methodically. "That's true. His brain is already traumatically damaged, of course. But it could worsen to the point that it would kill him."

"Well," Charlene said, glancing at Russell quickly for the first time. "Are the things you talked about in his head causing him to suffer more?"

"The hemorrhages?" Dr. Green asked. "That's just a fancy word for bleeding. I can't say if those two bleeds are causing suffering for him because I can't say that he is suffering. As we discussed this morning, he's virtually brain dead, like being in a deep sleep. I don't imagine he's aware of anything."

"And there's been no change in that?" Charlene asked.

"In his neural state? No, there has been no change."

"Oh God," Charlene said. "This is the shittiest thing I have ever had to deal with!" She turned and looked at Russell. "You hear me? This is the shittiest thing you have ever done to me." She wiped a tear from her eye, and her mom squeezed her arms for support.

Dr. Green placed a hand on the woman's shoulder. "I know all this is very tough."

"What has the hospital decided?" Charlene asked.

"No final decisions have been made yet. We want some time to pass. We have to give the patient time to stabilize, so we know exactly what his condition is. And perhaps most importantly, we have to give the family time to grieve and understand their options and the implications."

"I don't think we need more time," Charlene said, mustering a tough expression on her face. "Every minute this goes on is another minute of hell! He didn't think about us when he did this."

"Well, we don't want to jump to any decisions prematurely," Dr. Green said.

Charlene turned away from the doctor, folded her arms, and went to look out the window. Everyone found solace in the window, Eric observed, or maybe it was just an excuse to not look at other people. "No, my decision is the same as this morning," she said. "Let's not prolong his suffering. That's what he would have wanted."

Eric, who had been standing aside, listening patiently, spoke before he even realized it, "How can you say that? You don't know if he's suffering. He may pull through more than you realize!"

"Eric," Dr. Green said.

"Well, that's true, isn't it?" he asked.

Charlene turned in horrid shock and looked at Eric. Her lips moved for several seconds before she could find words to fill the air passing between them. "Excuse me?" Eric could tell she didn't know if he was a doctor or not.

"Please don't get mad at Eric," Dr. Green said.

"Who are you?" the still-annoyed woman asked.

Dr. Green stepped between them and answered for him. "Charlene, this is Eric Wright, he's one of the EMTs who rescued your husband this morning."

"An EMT?" she said. "And who are you to tell me what I should and should not do about my husband's life?"

"Don't blame him," Dr. Green said, speaking in a stern voice for the first time since Eric had met her. "He's a medic and therefore a patient advocate. He's trained to support life and only life one hundred percent of the time." Eric felt a small charge of electricity run up his spine. Dr. Green turned to him. "We can't afford to have our medics taking these nebulous debates out into the streets with them. That's not their job. But I do believe Eric was just about to leave." The good doctor looked at him with determined, gray eyes. Eric knew he had made an uncharacteristic outburst, and with just a few sentences, Dr. Green was able to explain why.

"I'm sorry," he said to Charlene. "That was uncalled for. I hadn't even officially met you." Charlene eyed him with continuing disdain and suspicion. He picked up his jacket from the chair; he could see it was time for Russell's one-day family to leave. "I guess I'll be going now," he said.

Dr. Green put an arm around him and walked him to the door. She spoke softly. "Eric, I'm sorry about that, but I don't think it's helpful right now to debate this woman. I enjoyed talking to you, and maybe you can visit later. But you've already done your job, and you did it well. I hope you know that. Just remember, you're the lucky one. You don't deal with ethics committees and lawyers. You get to fight for life, and you're going to be great at it."

Eric walked out into the parking lot feeling warm despite the chill. A small pile of dead leaves swirled in a cyclone across the concrete. Eric thought about Dr. Green's words after his outburst. He was the patient advocate, she'd said.

Patient advocates on both sides of this process would advocate different things for the good of the patient. One thing was certain—it was a long, complicated process, and people needed time. Out on the streets, there was no time. For ninety-five percent of the calls, life was the right decision, and there was no time to consider the other five percent. That was exactly how it should be.

Two days later, Eric and Tim brought a young woman to the hospital from a motorcycle accident. She was banged up but would be okay. Tim had a lot of paperwork to do and said it would be a while, so Eric asked if he could run upstairs to visit Mr. Baxter one last time. Tim rolled his eyes. "Okay, Eric. Just make it quick and listen to that radio. If those tones go off, you better have your ass down here in thirty seconds."

"I will."

Russell's room appeared just as it had before, but now sunlight flooded it. And Russell was alone. Eric had talked to Russell's current nurse briefly at the nurse's station. The situation had not changed. Dr. Green's prognostications about the end of Russell's life appeared spot on.

Eric drew back the curtain around Russell's bed. He, too, looked much the same, except the bandage on his head was smaller, and his head was turned in the other direction, toward the nightstand. There were no flowers or notes on the stand, just a silent phone. The only semblance of vitality in the room was the sound of the ventilator hissing as it pumped air through the tube in Russell's throat.

"Hey, Russell," Eric said. "I know you probably can't hear me, so I'm going to make this quick. I've been thinking about you a lot over the past couple of days. I just want you to know that I'm glad we had a chance to meet despite the circumstances, and I'm glad I was able to help." Eric tapped his fingers on the plastic bed rail and looked for a minute toward the sunlit window. "What I'm trying to say is that I know you didn't want to live anymore, and I know that it seems like no one else wants you to live anymore, either." The ventilator hissed and sounded mechanical, but it was the only voice Russell Baxter had now. No other movement or sign of life showed on his body. Eric paused and took a deep breath, then said, "I just want you to know that I want you to live. Even if that's not how things turn out, I at least wanted you to know that there was one person pulling for you. I wanted to thank you because you helped me realize that that's my job. I pull for everyone."

Joshua Keil is an officer in the United States Navy and an aspiring writer. While attending the University of Nebraska, he worked for three years at Rural/Metro Medical Services as an Emergency Medical Technician. In the military, he deployed to U.S. Military Hospital Kuwait as the Patient Administration Officer and more recently to New Orleans during Hurricane Katrina relief efforts. Joshua has been honing his writing skills since college. "Man Down" is his first piece submitted to a competition. The characters and setting are based on his full-length novel, Delaying Death. He lives with his wife and daughter in Hawaii.

Channel Two
by Robert Evenstell

It was easy to guess how he had lost control of his car. Rain, muddy dirt road, high speed, sharp turn. Now, his Jeep was sitting in the woods, all crushed and mangled. He might have escaped without serious injury, but while spinning off the road the Jeep hit the only big tree down there. Call it bad luck.

Apparently, Ashley got there first. Her red Chevy SUV stood not far from the place where the Jeep had slid off the road. Sarah had her Range Rover parked next to Ashley's Chevy. Ashley and I had been working together since the Emergency Medical Services started in Hallix two years ago, and we had known each other since we were kids. Sarah was the new girl on the block. She followed her fiancé to our quiet, rural town of 5000 and just recently joined our EMS squad.

By the time I arrived on the scene, the rain had settled down to a gentle, thin mist. I got out of my pick-up truck and walked around in front of it. There was no one on the road and no one near the crashed Jeep. I saw no one in the woods either.

Slammed against the tree on the passenger side, the Jeep had its driver's door flung open. What happened to the crash victim? Where have the girls gone? My watch showed 2:20 P.M. The dispatcher's call came at 2:00 P.M. It had taken me five minutes to get to my truck and fifteen minutes to drive there. So before I arrived on the scene, the girls had less than five minutes to . . . to do what?

Where are they? The question fogged my mind.

The subtle sound of wood hitting my car broke the eerie silence around me. I looked back over my shoulder. Just a pinecone. Something was amiss, though. There was no tree close enough for that pinecone just to fall on my car. It was a signal for me, but I didn't connect the dots. That's me, always a little late on putting two and two together.

Again, I looked around for the girls.

"Ash? Hey, Ash?"

"Get down!"

Sarah's voice came from somewhere close by. She was screaming as though someone's hands were squeezing her throat. Puzzled, I spotted Sarah lying on her stomach in the shrubs not far from the road. With the hood of her jacket put up, she waved her hand at me. "Duck!" The next moment came the gunshot. A bullet whistled close to me. Not that close—but close enough to shock me. I dived into the shrubs and lay still, my face down into the cold, wet, soggy grass.

"Are you okay?" Sarah's whispered. I didn't even hear how she crawled over to me.

"What's happening? Where is Ash?"

I barely recognized my own voice, muffled and flat.

Sarah whispered back, "Gathering some intelligence."

"Gathering what?"

"She went to find out who is shooting at us."

"Oh, no way! Don't you know the protocol?"

"Quiet! You talk–they fire!"

Sarah stared intently at the shrubs where Ashley supposedly had gone.

I was upset with Ashley for breaking the rules. Troublemaker! She knew too well that, under the circumstances, we should call the dispatcher, hide, and wait. I was upset with her but not surprised. Ashley earned her nickname for her forwardness and relentless drive for action. Her full name is Ashley Anna Adams, but we called her "Triple A" as in Always Ahead of All of us.

It suddenly dawned on me: "She might get herself shot any minute!" So obvious! All in a fluster, I was going to crawl towards the direction Sarah was looking. As soon as I made my first move, there was a quiet sound of rustling in the bushes, and then, much to my relief, I saw Ashley crawling towards us. She was well camouflaged. The colors of her jacket blended with colors of the late spring shrubbery. The hood of her jacket was pulled tight to her face, and only the tuft of her dark curly hair, almost flattened by water, was sticking out.

"Are you okay?" she asked me.

"You . . . " I was about to give her a little lecture, but Sarah interrupted me.

"What do we know?"

Ashley whispered back: "It's just one guy out there."

Ashley loosened the adjustment strap of her jacket hood. The soft darkness of the expanded hood surrounding her face emphasized the intense gleam in her eyes.

"The Jeep driver?"

"Apparently . . . He is injured, and he is calling someone on his cell."

"Calling whom?" continued Sarah with her questions.

"I couldn't hear it."

"Why did you go there? Don't you know the protocol?" I asked Ashley.

"We can't wait!"

"Why not—?" I asked.

"Did you check the car?" Sarah interrupted me.

"I did. It's empty."

"You sure?"

"I am."

That day, Sarah wasn't on duty. After Ashley had received the call from the dispatcher on her radio–and not everyone in our squad had radios–she was supposed to get hold of Matt. As I learned later, Matt had a family emergency, so, instead, Ashley teamed up with Sarah, who lived next door. It would have been her last choice because from the moment they met, Ashley did not get along very well with Sarah, calling her "beach blondie" behind her back. Listening to them talk, I could not help but notice that now they both were quite in rapport.

"Have you reported?" I asked Ashley.

"I told the dispatcher that I am on the scene."

"And then?"

"And then I lost them."

"No radio?"

"No radio, no cell, no nothing."

"Do they know?"

"They don't."

"Why don't you try again?"

"You try."

I did. All channels on my ICOM F14 radio were dead.

Except channel two, our internal channel. I heard Ashley. Ashley heard me and the whispering voices of two of us sitting in the shrubs. "What else could we expect, with short stubby antennas on both of our radios? Bummer!"

"Have you ever run into an armed criminal before?" Sarah asked me.

"A criminal?"

"Who else would shoot at the rescue team?"

"Why would anyone shoot at the rescue team? So strange . . . "

"We need to disarm him."

"Wait, you have already—"

"Randy, we can't wait!" Ashley almost said it aloud. "His next bullet could hit whoever arrives next. May happen any minute now."

True.

"I can do it," volunteered Sarah.

She would have had a good chance to succeed. Tall. Athletic. A professional lifeguard with proven record of "successful rescue under extreme surf conditions," her certificate reads. I would say, very successful. She once literally fished out her then-future fiancé drowning in the stormy waters of a Southern California beach.

"Let me deal with this guy myself," I said quietly, though in a stern voice.

"What's your plan?"

"You'll see. Where is he?"

"Over there."

"Where?"

I looked in the direction she was pointing.

"I don't see him. Do you think he crawled away?"

"No, he's still at the same spot. Next to that pine tree. Do you see him? Dark blue spot. Right over there . . . "

The pine tree she pointed at was about thirty yards away from us. "Oh yeah, now I see him," I pretended, still seeing no one. I did not want them to doubt me in any way.

Honestly, I wasn't excited about my mission at all. "Why don't we have long standard antennas on our radios?" I had been mulling the same thought over and over. "Our chances to call the dispatcher, to warn the rest of the team, and to avoid this missing in action adventure would be so much better." At the same time, I was glad that I had arrived before the girls got into that fight.

I took slightly to the right from the direction Ashley gave me. I was thinking to sneak up to his side or, even better, his back and to stealth-attack him. Crawling forward, I quickly learned to clear my way from the fallen tree branches, slowly putting them aside so that the sound of me doing that would drown in the usual sounds of the woods.

Everything was hazy in my mind; I was a mixed bag of emotions. After all, I had never dealt with an armed man before. Even armed with a knife. I didn't know how exactly I should confront this guy. Jump on him? Hit him? Lock his hand holding the gun, or hit him on the head with a tree branch? Something else? On one hand, I thought, no way that a car crash victim would be able to fight me, fit and tall, thirty years old, suddenly attacking him. On the other hand, I felt it bizarre that I had to fight the injured man, someone I was supposed to rescue.

After a while, I started to worry about crawling in the wrong direction. I still did not see him. Last thing I wanted was to become a point blank target of the armed criminal. The more I thought about the fight, the more easily my mind adopted the idea that he was an outlaw because subconsciously, I was looking for a good reason to justify me attacking someone who had been already hurt, perhaps badly. When I finally heard his voice, I felt relieved that I managed not to run into him accidentally. He didn't see me. He kept muttering something I wasn't able to hear clearly what. The next moment, I spotted him, lying near the tree, probably twelve to fifteen feet away. Dark blue jacket? Well, this was how Ashley saw it, for me it was more like gray. Was stress affecting my color recognition? He wasn't that big of a fellow; that was the only thing I was able to get. From where I watched, I didn't see his gun, and neither could I see his head, just his body behind the shrubs. He was muttering something, the same thing, over and over again. Yup, Sarah was right about that guy being a criminal. He was hoping to get help from his own rescue team. That explained why he was shooting at us. His phone was no different from ours, no signal, but things happen. A few short words could have gone through, and I didn't want to guess who would come to his rescue. I saw no other choice except to charge at him, the sooner the better.

I found a stone, heavy enough, and a good fit in my hand, a perfect weapon. It added to my confidence. "Action!" I made a couple more moves ahead, and then I heard him talking.

"Gunfighter 7 from Gunfighter 28. We've been hit. Gunfighter 7 . . . Anyone on the net?"

With those few words, the picture became clear to me. I started crawling back as fast as I could. The thought that I was about to attack an innocent, badly injured man overwhelmed me and made me less cautious in my moves.

Seeing me crawling back, the girls were ready for the bad news.

"What happened?"

"He is in shock. And he is confused."

They listened in silence.

"I don't think he is a criminal."

"Then who is he?"

"I guess he's from the military—a war veteran. Most likely from Iraq or Afghanistan."

"How did you figure it?"

"Gunfighter 7 from Gunfighter 28."

The girls knew enough about military radio call signals. Dorothy, our EMS chief, had come back from Iraq four months ago. She was there in the signal communication section, and from her stories, we became familiar with military radio talk. I didn't have to explain to the girls that the guy in the woods was calling his top Net Control Officer.

"He is still recovering from the brain trauma. He is disoriented. Doesn't understand what happened to him. Thinks that he is on the battlefield. Came under attack, and he is calling for help."

The girls were visibly relieved that we didn't have to fight an armed gangster, but we still had the same question to answer:

"What's next?"

The new knowledge didn't change our situation a bit. We still had a guy who would shoot at us if we attempted to help him, who would have shot at anyone who might have arrived, and who was in a desperate need of help.

Why did I crawl back? I should have disarmed him. I just wasted precious time! Thoughts burned through my mind like fire.

I was going to rush back, but Sarah quickly came up with another plan.

"Channel two!"

Her plan was surprisingly simple, so simple that I thought, How come I didn't come up with that myself? We were not all that sure that it would work, but we agreed on it without any debate.

After a brief rehearsal, I crawled back to the guy, the same way I did before. The goal was to get as close as I could and give the girls a signal. Ten feet, nine . . . eight . . . closer, closer. This time I came close enough to see him holding the phone. With my radio volume control turned up full, I leaned my hand holding the radio towards the guy to get an extra foot closer, and waited to raise my other hand for a "Go ahead!" as soon as I heard his gunfighter talk. He was silent. He didn't move. Did he lose consciousness? How long shall I wait? What if . . . ?

Then I realized that from the place I was lying the girls might not have seen me waving my hand because of the big tree right behind me. How else can I signal them? For a moment, I felt myself lost and helpless. I needed something I could throw, so they could see. And just when I needed it most, I didn't have at hand a tree branch or a stone, or even a pinecone, and I wasn't in the position to make moves looking for things around.

"Gunfighter 7 from Gunfighter 28 . . . Anyone on the net?"

With my free hand, I grabbed my baseball cap and sent it flying as high as I could. Sarah's voice on my radio came steady, firm, and loud, and the reception was very clear: "Roger. Gun-fighter 28, this is Avenger 16. Report. Over."

Would he answer? Please, please.

"Roger. We've been hit, over."

Holy smoke, it worked! He bought it!

"Roger that. Help is en route, over and out."

Darn! She was supposed to ask him about his location. That would be logical, that was how we had rehearsed it.

Why did she not just do that?

Well, anyway, now it was my turn to act.

I waited for about thirty seconds, and then slowly rose to my feet behind the tree. I didn't feel any fear while I crawled, but when I stood up a cold wave of weakness washed over me. What if he fires? With my knees bending and my hands trembling, I stepped ahead. Trying to get a hold of myself, I said loudly: "From Avenger 31 to Avenger 16."

He was lying with his face down in the grass, still holding his gun. His phone was lying nearby. He didn't hear me. He'd lost consciousness the moment he answered the radio, I guess. I even think that he had lost it before, the moment he had hit that tree, and only because of his extremely strong will power had he been able to keep his mind awake all that time.

The cops got there before we left for the hospital. Needless to say, we didn't press any charges against him.

His name was Wesley Stuart. We came to visit him once in a hospital. He was on his way to complete recovery. Wesley indeed had come back from Iraq almost a year before the accident. We didn't get all of the details, but his doctor briefly told us his story. Wesley was injured while on the reconnaissance mission when IED went off under his Humvee. He was the one who radioed for help. "Most likely," the doctor told us. "Wesley didn't realize that the operator took his call. It didn't register in his brain." Help came on time, but a burning hole was left in his mind. Ever since Wesley came back from Iraq, he'd been haunted by the memory of that day. His dreams turned to nightmares. He was diagnosed with Post Traumatic Syndrome Disorder and went through physical therapy, psychotherapy, and medications, but nothing worked. In his dreams, he was back in his wrecked Humvee. He saw his comrades dying, and he was calling for help, over and over again. In the middle of the night, he was jumping off the bed, screaming, falling, and hurting himself. The doctor said that as strange as it sounded, what happened in the woods that day was good for Wesley, for his mental recovery. Not the accident, of course, which cost Wesley two broken ribs, but the voice on the radio that he heard, Sarah's voice, telling him that help was on the way. That voice did what all his treatment programs failed to do. It filled the missing piece in the deep recess of his mind and put closure on his nightmares.

The horrors of his memories weren't holding him hostage anymore. Now, the doctor said, Wesley was finally getting his life back. "Call it good luck," the doctor told us.

Robert Evenstell is a freelance writer based in Orange County, California. He writes stories, novels, and screenplays and enjoys classical American and world literature.

A COMFORTABLE SILENCE
BY RAY WALKER

If you told Skipper Johnson he could get out of this meeting by gargling acid, he'd want a minute to think about it.

As chief of the Fairview Volunteer Fire Department for twenty-one years, he knew exactly what was in store for him that evening. He would present the town council with a budget he thought was fair, if not austere, and they would find reasons to nickel and dime it. Besides the gadflies who came to every council meeting, the only other people in the room were the librarian and the public works director who, like Skipper, were there to defend their budgets.

He was somewhere on Millstrom Lake, landing a seven-pound trout, when a commotion up front brought him back to the stuffy meeting hall.

"Chief Johnson?" called out Mayor Laurie Pyle. Nancy Niebeling, the librarian, was noisily packing up her things, red-faced. Now that the council had intervened, her budget no longer included her lone assistant or subscriptions to two dozen magazines. Nancy's position would be reduced to part-time, and the library hours would drop by a third.

Skipper waited for Nancy to exit before ambling to the front row. He landed heavily, and the ancient folding chair groaned in protest. "Good evening, Chief Johnson," greeted the mayor. She and the rest of the council looked weary. "As you may know, this is going to be an especially difficult budget year." Mayors came and went, but the script never changed.

"Then you liked my budget, I presume?"

The mayor raised her eyebrows, and Skipper braced for battle. "Yes, your budget is responsible. But we're cutting all budgets this year by twenty percent, across the board."

"Twenty percent!" barked Skipper. "That's impossible!"

Twenty percent was indeed draconian, but the town saw little choice. Fairview's economic engine was Appleton Industries, a hand tool factory that employed forty percent of the town. Within the previous ninety days, Appleton had lost its two biggest contracts, and the plant was hemorrhaging jobs. Tax revenues were projected to tank.

"I see you put in a fifty percent increase for diesel," said the skinny councilor on the end whose name Skipper could never remember. "That's quite a jump."

"Have you seen fuel prices lately? Fifty percent is probably too low."

"This new line item," said council president Lars Sandoval, who was elected before God invented dirt. "$10,000 for member incentives. What's that about?"

Skipper shifted in his seat. "I'm a purist: volunteer fire departments should be strictly volunteer. But we've been struggling to make calls lately, and folks're kind of down. I want to, you know, show them they're appreciated. The payments won't be much, maybe enough to fill their gas tank or put groceries in the refrigerator. Half my folks are Appleton employees about to lose their jobs, if they haven't already."

"That's a wonderful idea," said the mayor stiffly. "But if you add this program, you're going to have to cut back somewhere else."

"I put off new bunker gear 'til next year," answered Skipper. "That's where the offset is."

"This budget is higher than last year's," pointed out Lars.

"By only one percent!" said Skipper. "This budget stopped bleeding long ago; it's all bone now. I can't cut any more."

"I think you can," replied Lars sternly.

"All right," snapped Skipper. "I'll cut all my guys' salaries by twenty percent. No, make it fifty!"

"Chief Johnson!" scolded the mayor, glaring at him over the top of her reading glasses. She continued studying her copy of the budget while he looked on in slow boil. "I see that the fire department is scheduled to replace the ambulance this year." She looked up again. "Is that still the case?"

"Of course!" he answered testily. "That's from the sinking fund, though, not the town budget. The money's already there."

"Not necessarily," jumped in Lars.

Skipper scowled. "What do you mean 'not necessarily'?"

"The town has appropriated a portion of that fund for other purposes," answered Lars unapologetically.

"That money is for fire department capital improvements. It's not a piggy bank for your grubby little Swedish fingers—"

"That's enough, Skipper!" shouted the mayor. "Let's at least be civil about this. The money will be replaced, just not this year. The ambulance will have to last until then. It's only, what, five years old?"

"Eight," Skipper corrected. "And yeah, it starts most of the time."

Mayor Pyle didn't react to his implication. "The council will be meeting again two weeks from tonight. Please be here with your revised budget. We have an opening at . . . " She looked expectantly at the clerk.

"7:45," said the clerk.

"Laurie, I'm telling you, there's no way . . . "

"Chief Johnson, either you cut it or we cut it. This is your chance to do what's best for your department."

≈ ◇ ≈

Skipper was in a deep sleep, which was rare. Thirty-eight years on the department meant a full night's sleep was a luxury he almost never enjoyed. He heard the first set of tones, but he did not fully awaken. He was having a frightening dream, and the klaxon shrieking from his two-way radio was the submarine's decompression alarm as it plummeted helplessly to the bottom.

The re-tones woke him up, but it took a few seconds to surface from his watery nightmare. If the alarm had been Fairview's, he would be up with the first click of the dispatcher's microphone. But these tones belonged to Overlake Fire & EMS on the other side of the valley.

Overlake's tones were sounding a lot lately, and more and more of their calls were rolling over to Fairview. Grumpily, Skipper reached for his pants. When no one from Overlake acknowledged the tones, he knew what was coming. He was halfway down the stairs to the garage when Fairview's tones rang out. Overlake was out of service again.

"Wilton County Dispatch to Fairview Fire Department. Please respond to 1402 Amish Valley Road in Overlake for a sixty-eight-year old female, unresponsive." Skipper waited for dispatch to repeat the message and signed on responding. He opened the garage door and rolled down his driveway.

From dispatch, "Fairview, you got a crew?" No response. Skipper sighed.

"Randall, you coming?" he barked into his radio. It came out more harshly than he had planned. Randall was Assistant Chief and his most reliable responder.

Three miles away, Randall Hannity rolled over and crammed his pillow over his head. He'd been on seven calls that week, and it was only Wednesday. With all the layoffs, he'd been pulling a lot of overtime at the plant. He hadn't slept more than three hours in a row in two weeks. He'd promised his wife he'd shut off his pager that night, but he was so tired when he fell into bed, he forgot. "Randy . . ." exhaled his sleepy, exasperated wife.

"I know!" he snapped, shutting off the pager. He had a momentary, satisfying thought of heaving it across the dark room and hearing it smash into a thousand tiny bits.

Skipper approached the station, hoping to find at least another vehicle or two there, but the building was dark and lifeless.

"Wilton County Dispatch to Fairview, do you have a crew yet?" Skipper eyed the road in both directions, searching in vain for a set of wig-wags and red and white strobes.

"County from Fairview C-1," answered Skipper. "You better turn this one over to Shrewsville. I'll go directly to the scene and report back."

"10-4, C-1."

When Skipper arrived ten minutes later, the house was ablaze with light, radiating like a beacon in an otherwise dormant neighborhood. A frantic woman erupted from the front door, hollering into her cell phone. "The ambulance . . . no, just an EMT is here!" To Skipper, "Where is the ambulance?"

"It's coming," he answered calmly. "Where is the . . . your—"

"My mother! She's in the bathroom! Please hurry!"

The patient was lying on her back at the base of the toilet with her legs out straight and her arms resting neatly at her side. "Is this how you found her?" asked Skipper.

"No, I moved her. She was in a heap…" The patient's color was awful. There was already a waxy quality to her skin.

"Did anyone start CPR?" he asked as though he didn't know she was the only other person there. He kneeled to open her airway.

"No," she replied, choking on her words. "I couldn't . . . "

Skipper was almost through the second minute of CPR when the Shrewsville ambulance crew arrived. Neither EMT looked a day over eighteen years old.

"Where's your defibrillator?" he asked, winded.

"Oh, crap!" said one of them, turning to leave. "It's in the truck!"

"Use mine," growled Skipper, stopping compressions to attach two defibrillator pads to the patient's chest. He turned on the machine and said loudly. "Stand clear—analyzing!"

"No shock advised," said the machine. After the Shrewsville crew performed two more minutes of textbook CPR, the machine analyzed the heart rhythm again: No shock advised.

After the third No Shock, the crew backboarded the patient and fastened her to the stretcher, somehow managing to continue effective CPR the whole time.

At the hospital, an anxious-looking man appeared outside the emergency department entrance. "Is she going to be okay?" he demanded. Skipper was sure he'd seen the man before, on TV, maybe.

The crew pushed past him without responding and steered the stretcher into the building.

Overlake Fire and EMS had drill every Thursday night. On the first three weeks of the month, they practiced fire operations. The last Thursday was for EMS training, and as luck would have it, there were more school concerts, birthday parties and wakes in Overlake on the last Thursday of the month than at any other time.

When the number of EMTs among their ranks had dwindled a few years earlier, Overlake, and then Fairview, began to require all of its firefighters to become EMTs. Many resented the new policy, but because the department was a big part of their lives, they sucked it up and got certified. For them, fire was the prom queen; EMS was the nerdy half-sister who had to tag along on every date.

"You go on that code?" they asked each other at drill that night. The mayor's sister had died on her toilet, and they wanted details.

Trotter Johnson stepped out of the chief's office and hollered, "Okay, let's get started. Sevie's going to run things tonight. I have to leave in a few minutes."

The room was instantly filled with hoots. "How come you get out of drill tonight, Chief?"

"I gotta talk with Mayor Folbeare," he said solemnly. "Seems he wants to know why Shrewsville came for his sister from twenty miles out when Overlake's truck was parked three blocks away. He thinks maybe for the amount of money this town pays this department, we might be able to show up once in a while."

The room went numb. "Shrewsville took it?" asked someone. "I thought—"

"I was in Los Angeles," said Trotter. "I got back this afternoon. The first I heard of this was just now when the mayor called. Didn't any of you respond?"

He lost their eye contact. Suddenly the floor was the most interesting thing in the room.

"Cripes! It was the middle of the night!" he steamed. "You were home!" Throats cleared, but no one spoke. "Come on, guys! What happened?" Slowly the mumbled excuses came.

I had a sick kid. My pager crapped out. Dead battery. I slept through the tones.

I thought someone else had it.

≈ ◇ ≈

Trotter generally regarded Thomas Folbeare to be a gaseous windbag, but he sat quietly and listened to the mayor's grief-fed rant. He had no defense: his department had failed at a critical time, and he was prepared to accept responsibility. In a way, he was surprised it hadn't happened sooner.

Years ago, the community spirit was strong, and the three shifts at Appleton meant a healthy supply of volunteer responders at all hours. Then came more sophisticated medical interventions that required more rigorous training and testing. If patient outcomes were improving proportionately, the added demands would be tolerable, but they weren't. Trotter acknowledged his department was in trouble, all the more reason to admire the folks who continued to answer the call.

"And so," said the mayor, winding up. "I want to know what you'll do about this." Trotter hadn't really been listening.

"Do about what, sir?" The mayor grimaced.

"How do you plan to prevent this sort of tragedy happening again?"

"We need more volunteers," he answered. "Or we need to hire EMTs. My people are getting burned out."

"I hear Fairview has been having a rough time, too," offered Mervin Simp, the council's vice-chair. "My cousin runs on the Tindale Center Fire Company, and they get called all the time to Fairview."

"Maybe we could pool resources somehow," offered Charlie Clark. The proposal was met with blank stares. "Look, Fairview Fire Department has the same overhead Overlake has: worker's comp, equipment, supplies, vehicles, insurance, training. What if the two departments combined into one organization? That would cut costs, wouldn't it?"

All eyes fell on Trotter. "Uh, I don't think so," he said after a moment.

The mayor was nonplussed. "Why not?" he sputtered.

"Well, I don't think the Fairview Fire Chief would go for that."

"Isn't he your own brother?"

"Yes," said Trotter wistfully.

≈ ◇ ≈

Skipper lived alone in a saltbox house on the end of Forrest Street. At fifty-six, he was widowed; his only son, Cory, had been killed in a drunk-driving incident when he was only fifteen. Skipper had thirty-seven years in the Appleton plant, and when they offered buyouts during the previous downturn, he took early retirement. He did some contracting here and there, but by and large, the fire department was his life.

There had always been lean times when he wasn't sure they'd be able to staff an engine, let alone the other four trucks in the bay. The ambulance had always been the toughest to keep in service. Cutting up cars and running into burning buildings was one thing; treating mangled bodies and getting puked on was something else entirely. But new volunteers always came along, and the department managed to go on.

The department was shrinking, though, and lately it was the same seven or eight members who took all the calls. Now the town was trying to slash the hell out his budget. Aside from enduring the rigors of duty and time away from family, his firefighters were working with temperamental, outdated equipment. It made their demanding job more difficult, even dangerous. Worse, it sent the message that the town didn't care about them.

Skipper arrived at the next town council meeting just ahead of schedule, feeling completely at peace. His new budget would meet the council's demands; they could take it or leave it. Forty-five minutes later, Mayor Pyle summoned him to the front of the room without apology for the delay. He handed out copies of his new budget and waited. It was only one page, so it didn't take them long.

Mayor Pyle removed her glasses and gave Skipper a despairing look. "Is this some sort of joke, Chief Johnson?"

"No joke, your honor," said Skipper, stifling a grin. "You asked me to cut my budget by twenty percent. I did. If you think there is a better way, I am all ears."

"Skipper," said the mayor in a low tone. "Are you seriously proposing that we eliminate all fire suppression and vehicle extrication services from the budget?" Skipper nodded. "But . . . but that's what fire departments do!" she exclaimed.

"We're keeping the ambulance in operation," he explained. "EMS actually generates revenue through patient billing. The big red trucks don't earn us a dime, so I'm eighty-sixing fire operations. You'll have to contract for those elsewhere."

"Chief Johnson," piped up cranky old Lars Sandoval. "This is plain irresponsible and, and . . . childish!"

"With all due respect," said Skipper calmly. "The council is the one behaving irresponsibly. And you're the one having a temper tantrum over there, not me." Mayor Pyle couldn't resist smiling, and Skipper acknowledged it with a wink. "To expect every organization that's funded with town dollars to cut twenty percent is a mistake. I'm already at rock bottom. Diesel fuel, heating fuel, workers' comp, liability insurance—I can't eliminate 'em, and I can't bring 'em any lower. Trucks need regular maintenance, new tires, fuel. The apparatus bay needs heat, or the trucks will freeze up. And you tell me what it'll save us to drop insurance when someone gets hurt or killed." He looked severely at each of the councilors. "The only way I see to cut twenty percent is to get out of the firefighting business altogether."

The startled town council exchanged looks. "Chief Johnson," said Mayor Pyle. "This obviously is not acceptable." Skipper folded his arms and shrugged. "And the council does, in fact, have an alternative."

She held up a piece of paper. "This is from Mayor Folbeare in Overlake. It seems Fairview is not the only community in the county to be facing shortages for emergency services. They'd like to pool resources." A chill ran down Skipper's spine. "We ask that you confer with your counterpart at Overlake Fire & EMS to see how that might be accomplished."

Skipper's mouth went dry. "I'm afraid I can't do that, Laurie," he rasped.

Frowning, Mayor Pyle removed her glasses and slowly placed them on the table. "I beg your pardon?"

"I'm not willing to meet with the Overlake chief. I don't see how any cooperation is possible."

"He's your brother . . . "

"Yes," said Skipper. "But we don't speak."

"I'm sorry for your family problems, but that's hardly a concern of mine. Either you work something out with Overlake or find someone who will. You will be presenting your findings at a joint meeting with the Overlake council on December 6 at 2:30 PM." She placed her glasses on her nose. "We need to move on. I look forward to a report on your progress."

≈ ◇ ≈

Trotter and Skipper grew up on the waters of Millstrom Lake. When Skipper's son, Cory, was old enough to hold his own pole, he joined his dad and uncle in the boat. The three of them were fixtures on the lake, two men and a boy who idolized them both.

On a hot day in August, the year Cory turned fifteen, Trotter came by the house with his fishing pole. Cory and Skipper were staining the deck. "Go ahead," said Skipper to his son. "I'll finish this up. But be back by five."

Leaving Skipper behind gave the other two a surprising sense of freedom. Without the older brother and the father, rules could suddenly be bent a little. By the time they returned to shore that afternoon, Cory had wheedled from his uncle a few cans of beer and the keys to the truck. "You've had a few, Uncle Trotter," he said. "You better let me drive."

Skipper was the first on scene of the crash, the one who found his son's body in the ditch with a pick-up truck on top of him. Trotter sat in the road, unsure where or who he was, cradling an angulated left arm. Blood poured from a laceration on his forehead. The autopsy measured Cory's blood alcohol level at three times the legal limit for an adult.

Trotter pleaded guilty to reckless endangerment and was sentenced to probation, alcohol counseling, and a thousand hours of community service. He dreaded his brother's rage, yet longed for it, too, for only when it came and passed could the healing begin.

Skipper obliged, but only briefly, and it didn't pave the way to redemption. On the night of Cory's funeral, he tackled him and sent him to the emergency department for the second time in a week. After that, he tortured him with indifference, acting like he no longer knew him. He closed doors, crossed streets, and left stores rather than acknowledge his brother's existence. Trotter's guilt morphed into frustration, then rage, then hatred. Hatred ruled his life for years, destroyed his marriage, and cost him his job at Appleton.

Then one day, he discovered that he didn't hate Skipper, anymore. He had grown so accustomed to the distance, he'd simply stopped caring about him. At last they had something to share—indifference—and a comfortable silence settled between them.

Occasionally, they found themselves together on mutual aid calls, but they never let their personal difference interfere. They sent their deputies as go-betweens, and when the hoses were put away and the last truck cleared the scene, they went their separate ways without so much as a "see you later."

≈ ◇ ≈

By the time he got home from the town council meeting, Skipper's nerves were shot. He poured himself a drink, downed it in two swigs and poured another. A warm sensation settled in behind his eyes and down his cheeks.

He hardly ever drank—he had the stuff in the house for his poker buddies—and the two drinks went to work quickly. He flipped on the ball game, poured a third drink, and sank into his recliner. Fifteen seconds later, Fairview's tones blared over his radio.

"Wilton County Dispatch to Fairview Fire Department, please respond to 4 Nightingale Lane in the town of Fairview for a four-year-old male who is choking."

"Fairview C-2 responding." Randall was on his way.

"I copy Fairview C-2 is responding." Nobody else signed on.

"C-2, caller advises the patient has now stopped breathing. What is your ETA?" In the background, Skipper heard another dispatcher giving the caller instructions on clearing the boy's airway.

"I have an ETA of five or six," replied Randall. Skipper could be at the boy's side in two. He fought his way out of the recliner, and when he stood up, the floor tilted up at him. He stumbled toward the bathroom.

It took two tries to get the cap back on the mouthwash bottle. Teetering out of the bathroom, he slammed his shoulder on the doorjamb.

He climbed into his truck, threw on the red lights, and bounced over the curb into the road. Suddenly, there was blinding light and a piercing screech to his left. He crushed the brake pedal and turned his head. A hulking Toyota Tundra, still rocking from its sudden stop, was sitting close enough for him to reach out his window and touch its grill. He couldn't see the driver through the halogen beams.

"C-2," came dispatch. "Caller advises that the object has been dislodged, and the child's color has returned. Caller will bring the child to the hospital for evaluation. You are cancelled from this call."

Skipper waved an apology to the Tundra's driver and slowly backed into his garage. He sat numbly in his truck for twenty minutes, then closed the garage door and went to bed.

≈ ◇ ≈

The Overlake Town Hall was an historic building heated by clanging steam pipes and radiators that had a mind of their own. Regular attendees knew to dress in layers for meetings there. On this particular December afternoon, the temperature inside the meeting hall was eighty-five degrees. Outside, it was in the mid teens and snowing hard.

An arched window the size of a movie screen framed the Overlake and Fairview town councilors who were gathered around a long table in the front of the room. The large window revealed snow-glazed trees whipping about in the bluster and gave attendees the absurd sensation of roasting in the midst of a blizzard.

Town officials and emergency responders from as far away as Fair Haven had braved the whiteout conditions to be there, hoping the two towns had found a formula for streamlining emergency response systems they could replicate back home. The room was full but for two conspicuously vacant chairs in the front row. When the appointed hour arrived, Skipper and Trotter were nowhere to be found.

Twenty minutes later, the town clerk began to clear the sweating cheese slices from the refreshment table. The ice in the punch bowl had completely melted, so she took that, too. Someone else went to call the two chiefs.

After forty-five minutes, a red-faced Mayor Folbeare dismissed the assembly with his sincerest apologies.

≈ ◇ ≈

The number of college bowl games seemed to double every year, allowing lower and lower caliber teams into the mix. Not that Skipper minded. His recliner ranked high on his list of favorite places on earth, and with the storm raging outside, he was happy to doze in front of his TV while East Nowhere State battled Who's That Junior College in the Cooter's Bait Shop Cracker Bowl.

The sudden sound burst of a commercial startled him awake, and he began flipping channels. On the local government station, he recognized members of his own town council sitting dour-faced in the Overlake Town Hall. No one was speaking; the only sounds were dry coughs and squeaking chairs. The scene struck him as bizarre until a banner across the bottom of the screen explained all: LIVE: Joint Meeting of Overlake and Fairview Town Councils. "What the . . . ?" he thought, and then a smile crept across his face.

When he'd received the meeting reminder a few weeks before, he meant to inform the mayor that she was wasting everyone's time; he and Trotter were not going to meet. The notice got filed in the recycling bin. His ice fishing shanty needed repairs, and before long the meeting was forgotten altogether.

Trotter left nothing to chance. He was on a fishing boat in the Gulf of Mexico, not due back until after the first of the year.

≈ ◇ ≈

An ice storm on New Year's Day ravaged most of the trees in Skipper's yard. He unearthed his chainsaw from his cluttered tool shed, only to discover it would not start. Muttering that he should have replaced the beast long ago, he checked the classifieds for another one, grimly aware that he was hardly alone in this quest and would surely pay a steep price if he was lucky enough to find one.

He was already more than cranky when a quarter page ad on 7F caught his eye. The Town of Fairview is seeking vendor proposals for the delivery of fire and emergency medical services in its community . . .

Skipper put down the paper and called the mayor. "What's this about?" he snapped. He'd called her weeks earlier to apologize for missing the joint meeting, and although she had been a bit frosty, she didn't seem too upset, which surprised him. Now he knew why. "It almost appears you are looking for a new fire department."

"We are."

"But you already have a pretty good one."

"For now," she answered ominously. "We just want to see what options might be available."

"You can't just replace a fire department," he lectured. "It's not that easy—"

"We're not summarily dismissing you, Skipper," she cut in. "But you'll need to submit a bid."

"A bid? You aren't going to find a lower price tag than mine!" he shot back. "A fire department is not just another line item on the budget. If you close the library a couple days a week, no one will die. If I cut my budget any more, you're going to have to pick which days of the week we don't respond to calls."

Mayor Pyle didn't nibble. "Skipper, we gave you the chance to find some savings, and you stood us up. The revenues are evaporating. We have to find efficiencies everywhere we can. Now sharpen your pencil, and pitch us a winning bid."

He'd known Laurie Pyle a long time, and generally he liked her. She was tough, but fair and compassionate. Her hard line frightened him a little; perhaps the town really was in trouble. Still, he intensely resented her unwillingness to take him at his word. "You got my bid when I submitted my budget," he growled and hung up.

≈ ◇ ≈

When news of the Request for Proposals circulated, townspeople vilified the mayor and the town council. First Constable Billy Lowe had to hire two deputy sheriffs to remove protesters from council meetings. At the barbershop and bowling alley, townsfolk let Skipper know they were with him. Honestly, they agreed, who would try to replace a volunteer fire department?

Then a few things happened.

The town of Overlake issued their own RFP for fire and rescue services, and they made it clear that, if the voters of Fairview were willing, they would happily combine resources to sweeten the pot. The new service area would be forty-two square miles with eleven hundred calls and climbing every year. Overlake's auditor predicted overhead costs would go down thirty-five percent.

Appleton Industries announced it would be closing its Fairview plant in six months, prompting the town council to raise residential taxes by twelve percent in the next fiscal year to make up for the revenue shortfall. Mayor Pyle hinted that if savings could be found in the budget, the tax hike might not be so severe. Townspeople gently peppered Skipper with questions like, "You sure your budget is as lean as possible?" and "Maybe it's time you and Trotter worked something out, don't you think?" He responded patiently, but their fading support depressed him.

Toward the end of January, Billy Lowe arrived at poker with breaking news. "I was down to town hall this afternoon, and I heard the clerk telling Mayor Pyle we got a bid!"

"A bid?" asked Skipper. "For what?"

Billy handed Skipper a beer, which he turned down. "For a new fire department."

Skipper slapped down his cards. He'd been certain his "bid" was safe. He doubted any fire chief outside Wilton or Orange Counties would be interested, and all his colleagues at the recent Vermont State Firefighters' Association meeting assured him they planned no such takeover. Had one of them betrayed him? Billy had the answer. "It wasn't anyone I ever heard of. They're from Florida, I think."

"Florida?" sputtered Mugsy Thomason. "Do they even know what snow is?" Skipper didn't join in the laughter; he was deep in thought.

"I didn't get many details," Billy admitted. "But I gather they're not an actual fire department, just a company that contracts out fire and EMS all over the country."

"There are such things?" asked Alex Beaton. "That's a new one to me."

It wasn't a new one to Skipper. He'd been to national conventions, and the fire chiefs associations were all debating the concept. With a national headquarters and consolidated administrative operations, these corporations enjoyed efficiencies Fairview and Overlake could only drool over.

When the bidding period ended after a month, there were three offers on the table. Skipper and Trotter each resubmitted their budgets, and Titan Emergency Response Incorporated of Pensacola, Florida bid to take over both departments. The matter would be addressed at Town Meeting.

≈ ◊ ≈

The first Saturday in March was a gift to the winter-weary residents of Wilton County. After three solid weeks of smoky gray skies, chronic snow showers and sub-freezing temperatures, Central Vermont awoke to sun, blue skies, and temperatures soaring into the sixties. Cars got long-overdue scrubbings, neighbors visited on porches. The more adventurous heeded the call of the great outdoors and fanned out over land and water.

After an early supper, Skipper sat on his back deck to listen to jazz and watch the sun sink to the horizon. When darkness came, the temperature fell below freezing, and he returned to the comfort of his toasty house. He hadn't been inside two minutes when rescue tones drowned out the jazz.

"Wilton County Dispatch to Fairview Fire Department and Overlake Fire and EMS. Please respond to the Ketcham Forest trail head on Norton Road in Fairview for a report of lost hikers."

Skipper had left his truck in the driveway after washing it, and now a smattering of new-fallen snowflakes speckled its windshield. The thermometer on the dash read twenty-five degrees, and by the time he reached the station, the roads were coated. Winter had returned with a fury.

Fairview's Engine One was the first on scene, just seconds ahead of the Overlake trucks. Trotter's deputy, Sevie Hagridson, climbed out of the engine and approached Skipper. "Where do you want us?" he asked.

"Operations," said Skipper. Sevie nodded and returned to confer with his chief. Skipper was putting Overlake in charge of setting up the search and rescue effort. He tasked Randall with setting up a medical and rehab unit for returning searchers and, hopefully, the hikers.

A very concerned-looking couple approached Skipper. "Are you in charge?" the woman asked.

"I am," answered Skipper. "Do you know the missing hikers?"

"They're my twin boys," she choked between chattering teeth.

"Come inside my truck," he offered. "It's warm in there." Skipper was already getting cold himself.

"They're not really hikers," said the man after they'd settled inside the cab. "They're just two nine year old boys who went to play in the woods this afternoon."

"How were they dressed?"

"Just light jackets," sighed the mom, her arms crossed and her shoulders hunched. "It was so warm. They were supposed to be home by dark." Skipper hoped his face didn't reflect how alarmed he was.

"Approximately how many hours have they been gone?" he asked.

The parents looked at each other. About five hours, they guessed. Darkness had fallen an hour ago, and the temperature was forecast to settle into the single digits by midnight. Worse, the snow was getting heavier. Any tracks the boys might have left were long gone.

He shared none of this with the boys' parents.

The searchers' flashlights were hardly a match for the curtain of snowflakes enveloping them. At 2 AM, when frostbite started claiming tired, soaked firefighters, Skipper reluctantly suspended operations. Telling the parents of his decision was torturous. He knew all too well the helplessness and loss they were feeling, but the well-being of his troops had to be his first concern.

The mother said cruel things to him; the father made horrible threats, and Skipper absorbed their wrath with sympathy he hoped they'd never know themselves. There was still hope for their boys; perhaps they found a cave or other shelter. Perhaps they came out at the other side and are calling home from the warmth of a neighbor's house, wondering why they got no answer. Skipper ached to know what that would feel like.

"I'm very, very sorry," he said, relieved when the father finally led his wife to their car, glaring daggers at Skipper over his shoulder.

The search resumed early Sunday morning. The snow had stopped, but not before dumping another fourteen inches and concealing everything. Each white lump could have been a tree stump, a rock, a pile of leaves. Or perhaps a frozen nine-year old boy.

Search dogs were requested, but the nearest team was occupied eighty miles to the north. The soonest another team could be there would be Monday morning. Firefighters in tight rows cleared the ground as they marched, their adrenaline sapped by resignation.

On Monday, it took the search dogs less than half an hour to find the boys' bodies sitting entwined in a small crevasse between two enormous boulders. They had evidently pressed their tiny bodies into the gap for protection from the wind and snow, and in so doing let the frozen rocks rob them of their body heat. They drifted off peacefully, probably feeling cozy and warm near the end as the piling snow sealed their tomb.

≈ ◊ ≈

Town Meeting Day in Fairview was another beautiful day, even warmer than the weekend, but a palpable gloom hung over the residents as they filed into the elementary school gymnasium. A motion to postpone the meeting by a week was defeated; the will of the people was to get business done and over with. Few paid notice to the pair of well-dressed gentlemen sitting on the stage with the town council.

The assembly slogged through the first six articles in just over an hour, then Article Seven was read out loud: Shall the Town of Fairview enter into a contract with Titan Emergency Response, Incorporated of Pensacola, Florida to receive fire suppression, hazardous materials mitigation, vehicle extrication, and emergency medical services, for an amount not to exceed $98,960 with the option to renew said contract for two additional years at an increased cost of no more than 5% each year?

A yes vote, explained moderator Tiny Middleton, would mean the Fairview Fire Department would be replaced by Titan Emergency Response on July 1. A no vote would mean the town would retain the existing department and funding would be addressed in Article 8, the town budget. Tiny quickly got a motion and a second. "Before we start discussion of the motion, these two gentlemen from Titan would like to make a presentation."

Skipper rose. "Tiny, can I say something?"

The moderator gave a quick glance to the mayor. "Sure, Skipper. Go ahead."

Skipper turned to the audience. "You know me, and I know darn near all of you." Smiles and nods rippled through the room. "It's an honor to serve, and I'm sure all my guys and gals will say the same thing. It's harder to run a fire department these days than it used to be. We don't have enough volunteers. The training is demanding. I honestly believe the budget I gave 'em last fall is the best I can do. We give good service, and we love what we do. And I ask for your support. It's not just dollars and cents here, you know. It's about community, neighbors helping neighbors. I don't know anything about those fellows up there in the fancy suits. They may be somebody's neighbors, but they're not mine." He looked out at the crowd and saw approval. "I hope you think about that when you cast your vote. Thank you very much." He sat down to thunderous applause.

After one of the Titan presenters finished setting up a projector, the other strode out to the open area in front of the stage, rubbing his hands together. Not a single blond hair framing his tanned face moved.

"Good morning," he began in a robust voice. "It's a pleasure to be here today to tell you about Titan Emergency Response. My name is Frank Centers, and my associate over there running the projector is Gerry Mastiewicz. What we're here to tell you, and what we're going to tell the folks in Overlake later on, is that the world of fire and EMS is a rapidly changing one."

He cast a glance over at Skipper. "Your fire chief is a good man, I am sure of that."

"No you're not," muttered Skipper to himself.

"He has served you well for many years, am I right?" No response. "Am I right?" A solitary voice near the front finally said, "yes," and a few heads nodded.

"Of course, he has!" roared Frank Centers. "But fire and rescue services today need far more than he can provide you." An angry murmur stirred in the audience. "Don't get me wrong," Frank went on, holding his palms out. "I know it's not his fault, or anyone's actually. The best of the best resources are expensive, too expensive for a small town fire department to purchase."

"Like what?" someone asked.

"I'll show you, in just a few minutes. But first let me tell you a little bit about Titan Emergency Response." He was facing a sea of crossed arms, turned shoulders, and eyes pointed everywhere but at him, and if it rattled him, he didn't show it. Speaking with the polish of a seasoned salesman, he covered the basics of his company and the services it would provide.

For the most part, no one was really listening. Frank Centers's voice was a distant, sonorous drone in the background as they planned grocery lists and dreamed about warmer weather. And then he stopped talking.

Said nothing for ten full seconds.

Women looked up from their knitting. Men stopped doodling on their town reports.

On the large projection screen was a close-up of two beautiful, smiling boys: Tim and Tom Patch, the nine year old twins whose frozen bodies had been found just one day earlier in Ketcham Forest.

"I understand you all suffered a devastating loss over the weekend," said Frank Centers somberly. Not a sound, not a breath pierced the stillness. Seven hundred eyes were riveted to the screen where two happy boys grinned mischievously back at them.

The same photo had appeared in the newspaper. Some unscrupulous Tribune employee probably let it out, for a price, no doubt.

"I don't wish to cast aspersions on the dedicated folks who gave their all to the unsuccessful rescue effort," said Frank Centers, stepping closer to the front row and speaking yet softer. "They are heroes." By now, everyone was facing forward, absorbing his every word. "They simply didn't have the tools they needed."

A photo of a firefighter donning large mechanical goggles filled the screen, followed by a shot of lime green human-shaped images against a murky background. "Night vision technology is a critically important tool in search and rescue missions," he explained.

Next came a split screen: on the left, a photo of a forest in peak foliage taken from above; on the right was presumably the same forest, only it was a collage of blue and green splotches. In the center of the right-side image were bright yellowish-red shapes that were unmistakably human. "The photo on the right was taken with a thermal-imaging camera," said Frank Centers. "It detects varying levels of heat. Even in thick brush, temperature differences tell a very clear story. The good people of the Fairview Fire Department do not have this technology." He paused and delivered the hook: "But Titan does."

The next picture showed two dogs clad in bright green vests moving through a forest with their snouts close to the ground. "Titan also has teams of search dogs that can be deployed to any one of our units across the nation within twelve hours." He paused to let his words settle: the delay in getting search dogs to the scene was widely blamed for not finding the Patch boys in time.

Frank Centers concluded his presentation. "Titan is looking forward to adding Fairview to its growing family of community partners. I hope you give us your full consideration." A tepid, perhaps shell-shocked, applause rippled through the hall. "Are there any questions?"

"So," asked Martin Krabtree, rising and clearing his throat. "All of this comes as part of the package for $98,000? All inclusive?"

"Yes," said Frank Centers, stepping closer to Martin. "That is, presuming as per the RFP, all vehicles, equipment, and facilities currently in use remain in place."

Tiny Middleton waited a few more seconds and then asked, "Are there any more questions?" Members of the audience looked around at each other, but no one raised their hands. "Well, then, Mr. Centers, if you and Mr. Mastiewicz would be so kind as to step from the room, the assembled body will discuss your proposal."

"I await your decision," answered Frank Centers courteously. "We will actually be departing for Overlake now. Thank you for this opportunity." He and Gerry packed up their presentation materials while the room became a subdued din. As soon as they were gone, the moderator opened the floor for discussion.

Roger Kelly rose and turned to Skipper. "Chief, why is it that your department doesn't have any of this stuff?"

Skipper stood and faced the crowd. "Roger, these things cost a lot of money. I've been focused on getting the things we use all the time: foam for fire suppression, bunker gear, EMS supplies. The town, as you all know, has asked me to cut back, even on these necessities. Fancy gizmos just aren't in the realm of the possible."

Noting the unsatisfied looks of his audience, he went on. "We've never needed these tools for search and rescue before," he pointed out. "We've always found 'em with the gear we have. Would we have found these boys quicker with Titan's cameras and goggles?" He shrugged. "Don't know. Won't ever know."

He made his way slowly to the front of the room, suspecting more questions were coming his way.

Dudley Hampshire was called on. "Why is it, Skip, that Titan can afford this stuff and you can't? And why do they cost less than you?"

"It's economics, Dudley," answered Skipper, rubbing the inside of his ear with his index finger. "They're a national outfit that buys these things by the case and ships them to their field units. They get good deals because they buy so much. When little old Skipper from Podunk, Vermont buys one of this and one of that, little old Skipper pays the full freight."

"Does Fairview Fire Department have any plans to purchase this equipment now, given the recent tragedy?" asked Martha Pennington when she was called on. Skipper weighed all the possible responses, and decided to go with the honest one.

"No," he answered. "Those gadgets are just too expensive for our budget. You have to get the things you know you'll use all the time. Night goggles and thermal-imaging cameras would be nice to have, but we'd almost never use them."

A thoughtful silence fell over the room. "Is there any more discussion?" asked Tiny.

"I think the choice is clear," said Lars Sandoval from his seat on the stage. "With Titan Emergency Response, we can get everything we have today, plus a number of other features we don't have right now. And for several thousand dollars less than what Chief Johnson can provide it for. It's a fiscally responsible choice, and it brings greater peace of mind. I urge the body to vote yes."

Skipper wanted to be angry, to defend his department with indignation. But he was tired. Tired of fighting the single-minded town council. Tired of managing a shrinking pool of overstretched responders. Tired of getting up in the middle of the night. Tired of falling short of the mythical expectations of the community. Tired of giving it his all and still not being able to save those frightened, innocent boys.

As Tiny raised his gavel to close out discussion, Skipper raised his hand.

"Chief Johnson?"

"Thank you, Tiny." He faced the crowd and let out an enormous sigh. "Folks, Lars is right." The audience shifted in their seats and eyed one another. "I appreciate all the support you have given me and my department over the years, but the fact is, we can't compete with these guys. They're like, oh, say BMW, and I'm the guy making buggy whips. Maybe it's time we save the town some money and get better service. So go ahead and vote yes, if you want. Do what you think is best."

Maybe he was just imagining it, but he thought he saw relief forming on the faces nearest to him, as though he'd spared them some weighty dilemma. He glanced up at Lars Sandoval. The pompous old bat was looking straight ahead trying desperately to look like a gracious winner when inside, Skipper knew he was just busting with glee. "Anyhow," added Skipper as he returned to his seat. "I'm voting yes, if that helps any of you decide."

"So," said Tiny, gaveling the room quiet. "If there is no further discussion, I ask the question." He read the article once again. "All those in favor, signify by saying 'Aye'."

A large, unenthusiastic, "aye" filled the room. "All those opposed?"

A much smaller, but very loud group hollered, "Nay!"

"Any abstentions?" No reply.

"The ayes appear to have it. The ayes do have it, and the Article passes."

Frank Centers was equally persuasive with the people of Overlake. On July 1, Titan Emergency Response would add Vermont to its growing list of states.

"Did we make the right move?" wondered Mayor Pyle aloud in the empty gymnasium after Town Meeting. She had had her tussles with the crusty Skipper Johnson over the years, but she couldn't help wondering what he might be feeling just then.

"We're saving the taxpayers a lot of money, and they're getting better service," answered Lars. "Otherwise, I doubt anyone will even notice the change."

≈ ◇ ≈

The change was noticed almost immediately.

The Overlake Fourth of July parade was a century-old tradition, and nearly since the inaugural event, more than a dozen fire trucks from Shrewsville, Tindale Center, Overlake, and Fairview kicked it off with flashing red lights and barking air horns. Smiling firefighters and their kids threw handfuls of candy from truck windows while other members marched behind in crisp uniforms. The procession inspired awe and imagination in kids of all ages.

So it was a shock that July when only Shrewsville and Tindale Center showed up with three trucks between them with two self-conscious junior firefighters in T-shirts and shorts bringing up the rear. "Where are the Fairview and Overlake trucks?" someone asked.

"Not coming," answered someone else.

Back in May, Marci Jensen of the parade committee had contacted Titan's public relations department in Pensacola to work out the logistics. To her dismay, the Titan representative was unhelpful. "The use of company resources for non-emergency purposes such as displays, parades, and exhibitions, is prohibited," said the voice, a hundred and two years of proud tradition notwithstanding.

Titan didn't take part in the Fairview Town Party in September, either. For as far back as anyone could remember, the fire department provided the entrée for the event, a chicken barbecue that raised money for a different charity each year. Titan's absence might have been tolerable had the organizers found out sooner.

The day before the party, Eugene Lee, a member of the organizing committee, stopped by the station to inquire why the grills weren't yet on the town green.

"What grills?" answered Travis Ochre, the department's unit director.

"What do you mean, what grills?" A flummoxed Eugene Lee filled him in, and a light went on in Travis's head. Someone had stopped by a month ago and mentioned something about it. He'd checked with corporate, and to his relief, they said no. Didn't he get back to someone about it?

"No, you didn't!" said a stunned Eugene. "And everyone's counting on the chicken! The only other food will be salads and rolls!"

"I can appreciate that," answered Travis Ochre coldly. "But our employees can't be stuck behind a barbecue pit while their other responsibilities get ignored."

"You'll cut up some cars, at least, won't you?" asked Eugene.

Every year, when the food was mostly eaten, the crowd made their way to the parking lot in front of Town Hall for the fire department's extrication drill. Winners of a raffle got to sit inside donated cars and pretend they were injured patients trapped in the banged-up vehicles. While an EMT sat with them under a protective tarp inside the vehicles, firefighters removed the doors, windshields, roofs, steering wheels and seats. Freed patients were backboarded and moved to the ambulance for a ride around the green. The red lights and sirens were also the signal that the Rotary Club's homemade ice cream was ready for dessert.

"We won't be doing the extrication drill, either," said Travis dismissively. "We don't need the training, and we can't tie up resources like that. Besides, displays are forbidden in the contract. Sorry." He walked briskly to the door to show his uninvited guest out.

Efforts to find enough meat and grills to replace the fire department's barbecue came up short, and the crowd tried to make do with the pasta salads, chips, and rolls. With no extrication exercise to occupy them, they milled around until the Rotary's industrial sized ice cream makers finished making their dessert.

"I never realized how much the town party revolved around the fire department," someone observed.

"The parade was pretty lame, too," someone else added. The town party usually started with a fire truck parade, a half-mile route from the White Pines Campground to the town green. Kids painted their faces, decorated their bikes and rode the parade route behind the big red trucks. This year, without the fire department, the parade lost much of its glamour. One person pointed out that the kids on bikes looked just like any other summer day on Main Street.

October was Fire Prevention Month, something Skipper had always taken very seriously. He and a few of his firefighters had visited the elementary school each week with a new theme: don't play with matches; stop, drop and roll; make an escape plan with your family; change the batteries in your smoke detector.

Titan refused to participate in the school program, of course. Corporate headquarters was kind enough to ship one-hundred fire prevention calendars to the school, a lukewarm gesture given there were four-hundred students in the school. Skipper had always parked a different truck on the playground each week for the kids to climb all over at recess. Titan? No chance.

Community outcry over these snubs grew so great, Mayor Pyle summoned Travis Ochre to a town council meeting in November. He seemed puzzled by the ferocity of the complaints and answered each with a passionless defense of his company's position, citing legal and practical concerns.

"Entertaining you is not part of our job," he said severely. "Emergency response is a business, not a frivolous side show to inspire your boring lives. We are first and foremost an emergency response system that must remain ever ready to save your lives and property at a moment's notice." Rising from his seat, he added, "If there are no questions, I have to get back to the station to keep the backup ambulance in service. Good night." Without waiting for a reply from the stunned council, he left the room.

≈ ◇ ≈

For Skipper's entire adult life, he lived with vigilance so constant, it was subconscious: he checked his radio's battery level more often than his watch; left the house occasionally without his wallet but never without his pager; used the toilet when he thought of it, not just when he needed to. At any moment, a crisis might erupt in Fairview, and it was up to him to mitigate and stabilize it.

After a few unsettled weeks of waking up to phantom tones and reaching for his non-existent pager, he gradually adjusted to a responsibility-free life. Once he turned the corner, he had no desire to look back. Perhaps he should have stepped down a whole lot sooner.

His former members were less happy with their newfound freedom. Several sought jobs with Titan and excelled at the strength, agility, and operational tests. They just couldn't get past the personality inventory. "Lots of questions about killing animals," complained Randall at poker one week. "They even asked if I wanted to kill myself! It was a creepy test."

Though the company was not in line for any congeniality prizes, Titan scored high marks during its semi-annual review by the Overlake and Fairview town councils. They'd established a response plan with one ambulance in each town. If one was on a call, the other stood ready to cover both towns. By keeping crews at the station instead of responding from home like the volunteers did they cut the average response time in half. In six months, only two percent of their calls were turned over to outside agencies, and then only because both of their rigs were already on calls.

≈ ◇ ≈

Millstrom Lake, a seven-square mile body of water, formed the southern boundaries of Fairview and Overlake. For years, Skipper and Trotter fished it for trout and walleye in the old rowboat they'd inherited from their father. Old man Johnson also had a small camp at the north end, just about where the two towns met, and the brothers once spent lots of time there.

After Cory died, Skipper built his own bundle of sticks on the opposite shore. If Trotter still used the old place, he didn't know or care. He spent his new-found free time winterizing his shack. He was practically living in it by the time the snow came.

January was brutally cold, but the first day of February arrived with a blast of warm air. At 8 AM, it was almost forty degrees and climbing. There was no breeze, and the sky was a deep, rich blue. Skipper's was one of dozens of shanties that dotted the lake, but he was the only one fishing that morning, and the world was silent. Sitting in a canvas deck chair on the open ice instead of huddling inside his shanty, he leaned back and enjoyed the sunshine on his face, fishing line in one hand and a mug of coffee in the other.

A familiar noise from inside the shanty broke into his reverie: Titan-Overlake Rescue tones. He kept his radio in the shanty as a buffer from the occasional loneliness that ice fishers both crave and dread. The cadence of the chatter and the order in which calls usually unfolded were as familiar and comforting as an old quilt on a chilly night.

Sitting twenty feet from his closed shanty, he couldn't make out the address or the nature of the call, but he didn't really care, either. As usual, Titan signed on in less than a minute, and Skipper tuned out, preferring his meditative state. He considered turning off the radio, but it seemed like too much work to stand up and walk all the way over there.

Silence continued for several minutes, and then a new wave of chatter erupted. Skipper couldn't hear the words, but the tenor reflected distress. There was a rapid exchange between dispatch and the Titan crew, and curiosity got the better of him. He extricated himself creakily from the low-slung chair and limped into the fishing shanty.

"County from Titan-Overlake. Our GPS shows the address is on the west side of the lake."

"Negative, Titan-Overlake," came dispatch. "347 Moccasin Lane is on the north side, off Kingfisher Way."

347 Moccasin Lane was Skipper's dad's place. Trotter's camp now. Skipper felt a tiny burst of adrenaline in his chest.

"Titan-Overlake, are you ready for a patient update?"

"Affirmative." While the Titan microphone was open, Skipper could hear shouting in the background. Perhaps the crew was debating which directions to follow: County's or the GPS?

"You have a fifty-five-year old male complaining of chest pain. Seven out of ten. Started when he woke up this morning." Trotter was fifty-five. Through the rest of the update, Skipper pictured his brother in their dad's beat-up camp, sitting on the couch and clutching his chest, terrified. He'd fantasized about this sort of thing

146

before. Gratifying in the hypothetical; the vision brought no satisfaction now.

"Thank you, County," replied the Titan-Overlake crew chief. "Uh, we're still not finding Kingfisher Way on our GPS. Can you give us cross streets?"

"There are no cross streets," answered dispatch patiently. "Stand by." A few moments passed. "Titan-Overlake, from highway 242, take French Road at mile marker 17. At the end of French Road, turn right onto Kingfisher Way. Moccasin is .7 miles on the right."

"Route 242?" came the anguished reply. "We're on Route 18! Our GPS mapping told us to take 62 to 18!"

Route 242 was three-quarters of the way around the lake from Route 18, fifteen minutes under the best of circumstances. Snow covered most of the winding dirt roads to the camps. The eight-ton ambulance might not even reach Moccasin Lane.

Dispatch re-directed the ambulance then added, "Be advised that we've lost contact with the caller. The line remains open, but he has stopped responding."

Skipper later had no recollection of hopping onto his four-wheeler and zipping north across the frozen surface, homing in on his father's old shack. His mind cleared when he found his brother lifeless on the sofa. He scooped up the phone, announced his arrival to the dispatcher and started CPR.

The last time he was on top of his brother like this, he was trying to kill him. Now, without knowing why, he was trying to save him, screaming at him to do something to help. "Don't just lie there, you lazy son of a bitch!" Almost eight minutes had passed since Trotter went unresponsive. Odds were long and fading.

Skipper finished a set of chest compressions and prepared to breathe into his brother's cyanotic lips again. Trotter's limp features evoked innocence and vulnerability and brought Skipper back to the summer when they were twelve and eleven.

The boys were swimming across Poor Farm Bay, the wide bowl of water where their father's shack sat. The strong current wore Trotter out, but he wouldn't quit. Skipper swam as hard as he could—he wanted to crush his little brother's will—and he went limp after reaching shore in personal-best time. He rolled onto his back to assess his margin of victory, but all he saw were ripples. A small hand popped out of the water, then disappeared. Aided by the current, and re-energized by adrenaline, Skipper retrieved Trotter's motionless body and hauled him back to shore.

Then and now, Trotter looked so much younger that he was, so helpless. Skipper managed to bring him back that summer, but this time Trotter's heart, not a lungful of water, was the culprit, and so much time—too much—had elapsed since it last beat.

Tired after several rounds of CPR, Skipper picked up the phone to see if dispatch had an ETA on the ambulance. They did not. He resumed CPR, his anger building as his brother's chances faded.

The next time he switched to respirations, it was Cory he saw in his brother's peaceful face. The boy looked so much like Trotter, the brothers often joked in friendlier times about which of them was his real father. When rescue crews had finally pulled Cory's broken body from beneath Trotter's pickup, it was Skipper who managed his airway, refusing to step aside even when others resorted to rudeness. He breathed for his son the whole way to the hospital. There, it took three security officers to wrestle him off so the emergency department could take over.

Skipper placed his hands back on Trotter's sternum and began pumping vigorously, much faster than protocol dictated. Rage he couldn't fathom made his eyes itch and his nose tingle. A lump formed in his throat, and his chest heaved. He drew in a deep breath and began to wail, releasing deep stores of anguish he'd long ago packed away and forgotten. He bellowed at his brother, berated him until his words disintegrated into meaningless syllables. Tears rained from his eyes and left widening circles on his brother's shirt. He could barely breathe for the sobs. All the while, he continued the violent compressions, but respirations became impossible.

Eventually the Titan crew arrived, and when the defibrillator was ready, Skipper moved to a chair and watched, drained.

"Stand clear!" ordered the calm voice on the machine. It then emitted an ascending slide whistle tone while it charged up to deliver a shock to Trotter's heart.

The pronouncement startled Skipper. Trotter had been lifeless for at least twelve or thirteen minutes. He couldn't have a shockable rhythm. The machine surely was misreading his cardiac activity.

"Stand clear!" said the crew chief, who was running the defibrillator. Trotter's body twitched from the shock. After two minutes of CPR, the crew chief hit the Analyze button, and the machine wound up for another shock.

"Stand clear."

After two more minutes of compressions and breaths, one of the EMTs palpated Trotter's carotid artery. His face registered amazement; he fingered Trotter's wrist for confirmation.

"We've got a pulse! Let's move!"

While they wheeled the stretcher up the snowy path and into the ambulance, Skipper gave them what little he knew about Trotter's medical history. He declined their offer to let him ride along, using the logistics of retrieving his four-wheeler as an excuse.

Trotter's heart kept beating all the way to the hospital. An hour later, he was still alive, in surgery receiving a triple by-pass.

Skipper found himself in Trotter's room the next day, not certain why he was there. His brother's survival was miraculous; perhaps he just wanted to see it for himself.

Trotter looked like a rag doll propped up in bed with a vent tube crammed into his mouth. His body heaved with every inspiration, reminding Skipper of the manikins their father used to rig on the porch every Halloween. Attached by fishing wire to tree branches, they moved when the wind blew and scared the pants off trick-or-treaters.

He returned the next day and sat with him for a while, staring incredulously at the steady beats registering on the heart monitor. A nurse was changing the IV when he arrived on the third day. The ventilator was gone, replaced by a non-rebreather mask, and Trotter's posture wasn't as limp.

"He looks better," Skipper said to the nurse. "How's he doing?"

The nurse looked up at him. "Why don't you ask him yourself?" Trotter's eyes fluttered and opened a crack, his lips crinkled in a weak smile behind the plastic mask. Slowly, he nodded and tried to speak, but by then, Skipper was gone.

≈ ◇ ≈

In mid-February, Titan Emergency Response informed the town councils that they would need to adjust the second year of the contract upward by forty percent. If the towns could not collectively add about $80,000 to their emergency services budgets, Titan would pull up stakes and leave. Travis Ochre quoted the language in the contract giving Titan the authority to make such a demand.

The driving force in the increase was an alarming drop in revenues. The number of uninsured patients skyrocketed when Appleton Industries left, and none could cover the costs out of pocket. Unless the towns could cover the shortfall, Travis said, continuing to do business in Wilton County would no longer be feasible.

"You could do a chicken barbecue," joked Mayor Pyle, but Trevor Ochre didn't so much as smile.

≈ ◇ ≈

Since Titan was demanding more than the five percent increase stipulated in the previous year's article, the contract renewal was put before the voters at Town Meeting and rejected without discussion. There was a better offer on the table, one that arose from a passing comment made months earlier.

Over beers after a Fireman's League softball game, someone joked that Tindale Center and Shrewsville ought to merge their fire departments so Titan couldn't add them to their empire. The notion gained traction, and in September, serious discussions broke out. By Town Meeting Day, the following article was put before the voters: Shall the voters of Fairview, Tindale Center, Shrewsville and Overlake approve the formation of the Southern Wilton County Emergency Response Corporation and contract with said corporation for fire suppression, hazardous materials mitigation, vehicle extrication, and emergency medical services for an amount not to exceed $25 per capita for the coming fiscal year?

Randall Hannity, who was chosen to head this new corporation, explained to the Fairview voters how the four communities would share resources, coordinate more efficient responses and collectively negotiate deals on equipment and services once beyond their reach.

No, he explained when asked, the new corporation would not exclude itself from town events, and in fact, a Shrewsville firefighter had a delicious barbecue recipe they would debut at the next Town Party.

The article passed on an enthusiastic voice vote.

≈ ◊ ≈

Skipper heard the knock on the door, but decided not to answer it. May 5th was a hard day–this would have been Cory's thirty-second birthday–and the steady rain didn't help. Then he remembered: Randall was coming by that afternoon to pick up some paperwork. Reluctantly, he got up and opened the door.

Trotter wasn't dressed for rain. He looked pathetic standing on the front stoop getting drenched. Skipper stared cross-armed for a moment, then stepped back in a non-committal invitation to come inside. Trotter obliged and closed the door behind him.

"I won't stay," Trotter announced, squeezing his hands together. "I just thought . . . I wanted to . . . " Skipper shifted his weight, but his face betrayed nothing. "I figured it was time I should, you know, thank you in person for saving my life." No reaction. "Well, that was it." He turned reluctantly for the door.

Skipper finally spoke. "Don't count on me doing it again."

Trotter rested his hand on the knob for a long second then opened the door. A firm hand on his shoulder kept him from leaving.

"The next time you get chest pains, would it kill you to pop a mint or two in your mouth?"

Trotter scowled over his shoulder. "What?"

Skipper was glaring at him. "It damn near killed me to put my mouth on that smelly maw of yours."

Trotter stared. "Whatever," he sighed at last, stepping onto the stoop.

He looked out at Skipper's soaked front lawn. The door didn't shut behind him. He spun around.

"You do crappy chest compressions, you know that?"

Skipper's stony façade began to crumble, bested by Trotter's quirky sense of humor.

"I've got a fire going in the other room." He crooked his finger. "Come on, you look like a drowned raccoon."

≈ ◇ ≈

Two old men sat in a battered wooden rowboat staring at the ripples spreading from their fishing lines. Conversation, when it happened, came in short snatches: last night's ballgame, a joke heard at the barbershop, war stories from the helm of Engine One. Mostly, they sat and fished in comfortable silence, sometimes letting an hour or more go by without uttering a word.

The weightier matters of the boy's death and their long estrangement were never brought up, a condition of their tacit peace accord. It was pragmatism, not stubbornness or fear that steered them from these murky depths: dredging up pain and sorrow would not bring Cory back.

In their memories, though, the boy was very much alive, happy and forever fifteen. While they fished the pristine waters of Millstrom Lake, side-by-side in a rickety old boat, there were three of them again, two old men and a boy who, after all, still adored them.

Ray Walker moved from Honolulu to Vermont in 1974. After graduating from the University of Vermont, he worked in advertising and insurance before accepting a position on the staff of Governor Howard Dean, M.D. in 1992. Since 2000, he has been the EMS Programs Administrator for the Vermont Department of Health, where he oversees the testing and certification of EMS providers throughout the state. In addition to his administrative role, he volunteers as an EMT with the Charlotte Volunteer Rescue Squad. He enjoys biking, hiking, kayaking, snowshoeing, cross-country skiing, traveling, and writing (music and fiction). "A Comfortable Silence" is his first publication.